The
BOOK OF DARRYL

Interpreted by The Goggles
and Matthew Bate

Illuminated by Scorpion Dagger

Musical Stylings by
Ryan Battistuzzi

* * *

MCD

Farrar, Straus and Giroux
New York

MCD
Farrar, Straus and Giroux
120 Broadway, New York 10271

Library of Congress Cataloging-in-Publication Data
Names: Goggles, author. | Bate, Matthew, author. | Scorpion
 Dagger, illustrator. | Battistuzzi, Ryan, contributor.
Title: The book of Darryl / interpreted by The Goggles and
 Matthew Bate ; illuminated by Scorpion Dagger ; musical stylings
 by Ryan Battistuzzi.
Description: New York : MCD/Farrar, Straus and Giroux, 2021. |
 The Book of Darryl is based on an online series of the same
 name.
Identifiers: LCCN 2020042289 | ISBN 9780374115319 (hardcover)
Classification: LCC PS3607.O34478 B66 2021 | DDC 813/.6—dc23
LC record available at https://lccn.loc.gov/2020042289

Designed by Alex Merto and The Goggles

Our books may be purchased in bulk for promotional,
educational, or business use. Please contact your local bookseller
or the Macmillan Corporate and Premium Sales Department at
1-800-221-7945, extension 5442, or by email at
MacmillanSpecialMarkets@macmillan.com.

www.mcdbooks.com • www.fsgbooks.com
Follow us on Twitter, Facebook, and Instagram at @mcdbooks

10 9 8 7 6 5 4 3 2 1

Contents

* * *

o fully engage with this book, point your phone's camera at this freaky symbol. It downloads an app that makes the pictures come alive when you point your phone at them.

Sick, right?

SUMMER

arryl was minding his own business waiting for his mom to come out of the tunic store, feeling bored as he hovered near the side of the building and gazed deeply into his phone, when someone or something bumped into him. A casually mishandled backpack? A bro shoulder? Hard to tell, except the bump felt concentrated, intentional — somewhere between a hard nudge and a light shove, which was strange considering there couldn't have been anyone behind him.

Whatever. The bump sent his phone flying out of his hands even though he'd been clutching it like it were a string of worry beads. But when he bent over to pick up his phone, his stomach felt weird; it lurched and then hung sickeningly suspended, like he was falling. Then he realized he *was* falling, but from way up high, which was also weird since he hadn't been way up high just a second ago — or ever

in his life, really, since being way up high was the worst.

Even weirder, he seemed to be falling from a tree.

Darryl hadn't been in a tree, he didn't much like them, but he had a hard time focusing on this little fact as he plummeted to the ground. Instead, his eye was caught by something rushing toward him through a blur of passing leaves and branches, and then he recognized that the something was a someone walking up the middle of the tree, his face coming into focus as he rushed past: Wade!

Darryl hadn't seen Wade in forever. Not since Wade had died, in fact. Darryl smiled and waved, but Wade didn't seem like he was in a smiling or waving mood, and then he was long gone. Then Darryl sped by himself on a branch, watching himself fall, tree-branch Darryl waving and smiling at falling Darryl. And then he began to spin.

It was a nightmare, of course. Ever since Wade

Figure 1
"And Then He Began to Spin."

died, all he'd had were night-
mares. Still. There was something different about this one.
He continued to spin, faster
and faster, and the images
whizzing past him got less
and less recognizable—a raven,
bulging eyes staring deep
into his soul, a banner with
his name emblazoned across
the top of it, flapping in the
wind, a version of himself he
didn't recognize, who then—
somewhat surprisingly—
burst into flames. Images and
scenes full of faces and sounds
and feelings, at once familiar but off, like the record-
ing of his life had been sped
up and blurred together. The

Figure 2
He Reached for His Book That Was Actually a Binder.

nightmare engulfed him. He'd never been so engulfed in anything, certainly not in this flyblown desert town where nothing ever happened, certainly not in the middle of the least eventful summer of his entire seventeen years of life. It was the freakiest, most intense ride his subconscious had ever ginned up, and that was saying something.

They say your life flashes before your eyes at the end, but what if the life that flashes before your eyes is one you don't recognize? Does that mean you're at the beginning? Sadly, except for the falling bit, Darryl didn't remember a

lick of it when he woke up, was left with just an overwhelming sense of sadness, loss, and . . . elation?

And finally, peace.

Elation was weird, but it was the peace that really got to him, that made the dream something he needed to tell someone about. But who? And then, in the retelling, he would only screw it up. Who can articulate the alchemical magic that happens in a dream or nightmare ("And the camel had teeth, but, like, *human* teeth!") and that makes a dream so terrifying, mysterious, and annoying for others to hear?

If he had a BFF, he'd probably just mention it casually while they were shooting hoops or whatever, but he didn't, not since Wade, so, whatever. Instead, he reached underneath his bed for the very next best thing: his book. It wasn't actually a bed per se, since he didn't have one of those either, only the very rich had beds — it was actu-

ally a blanket on top of some barn boards that Darryl had fashioned to look like what he imagined a rich person's bed looked like.

His book wasn't actually a book either. It was a binder, and actually, after all these years it looked less like a binder than it did a cabbage, its pages plumped from endless thumbing, its cardboard binding softened from his sweat (and tears, quite possibly a few tears). It contained pretty much all of his thoughts. Confessions for his eyes only. Some pretty powerful poetry. Musings. Things that made him less than happy. Significant investigations.

He also called it a book because the therapist who had given it to him after their first session had said, "Darryl, there's no way you're gonna be able to deal with all your issues, so maybe, in addition to bottling them up inside you, put them in this book too." And Darryl took it, thinking, It's a binder, not a book. But he

had to admit, a book sounded like a way cooler place to keep his innermost thoughts. He'd written "The Book of Darryl" on the back cover and traced over it again and again while thinking that not only was a book way better than a binder, it was way better than a friend, since it was always there, ready to listen or be drawn upon. All you had to do was keep it safe under your fake bed.

A sleeve on the inside back cover held a little ruler, which was handy for when things needed measuring.

He flipped to a tab labeled DREAMS. The page was empty save for a crude drawing of a camel with oversize human teeth. He tried to think of the peaceful feeling that had come across him after he woke up as something liquid washing over him, but that was hard to convey in words, and then he tried to capture the fear and the loss and the sadness, but when he looked at the page and saw that all he'd done was write down "fear" and "loss,"

followed by a frowny face, he gave up.

Instead he flipped back to the section labeled WADE.

In all of his life, Darryl had had one good friend. Wade.

It was fourth grade. Darryl felt like he was going to puke. Darryl, by then, was an expert at puking. He knew all the signs: tingling glands, heavy head, an overwhelming sense of impending shame. He was in PE, which was #1 on his list of Worst Times/Places to Puke. He had to move.

He shot out of the gym and ran for the locker room, hands over his mouth, full, really full of pre-puke — mostly saliva, but, like, the spicy kind. As he reached the bathroom door, the next blast filled his closed lips to the brim. Darryl could see the safety of the locker room through the small window above the doorknob, the long fluorescent bulbs flickering under their wire-cage covers.

As soon as he pushed through the door, he let fly.

Figure 3
It Was Mostly Saliva, but, Like, the Spicy Kind.

✳

All over some kid he'd seen only once before. The kid cocked his head and looked at Darryl and then down at the puke all over him. He shrugged and held out his puke-covered hand and said, "Hey. I'm Wade."

Wade skipped his next class and helped Darryl clean up the mess, which wasn't so bad, since Wade had somehow instinctually held his shirt like a scoop to catch most of the spray. Wade wasn't a big talker, but it was nice to have company.

They sat together at lunch, and Wade reassured Darryl that he'd almost made it, a

Figure 4
"Wade's Dad Sat on the Couch All Day."

few more steps and no one would have known. "So close!" Then Wade told him about how he had once puked at his grandma's house after a funeral, all over her nice couch, right after she'd taken off its cover for the first time ever. "The couch, it had been, like, waiting for this moment, like, its coming-out party." He took a sip of warm milk from his goatskin. "I mean, without its shell, the colors seemed kind of sad? But who cares, right? Because, like, for one day, it had been free? Even if it did get puked on. Worth it."

Wade was cool, although it was hard for Darryl to

articulate why or how — even in the paper privacy of his binder. He could never come over to Darryl's house. Darryl could only ever go to Wade's house. And when he was there, Wade's mom wouldn't let them eat sugar. She wouldn't let them eat chocolate either, only carob, which was even worse than the baker's chocolate Darryl used to sneak out of his mom's cupboard. This was maybe because Wade's dad sat on the couch all day drinking diet mead he'd added extra honey to, and when Darryl came to visit, he'd sometimes use his tongue to wiggle inside his own mouth and pull out a tooth and drop it into a jar.

Even though Wade was considerably smaller than Darryl, and Darryl himself never realized it, Wade was always very protective of him. Like when they crossed the street, Wade would hold him back, look both ways to make sure the coast was clear — even though the coast was always clear — then usher Darryl across. Or sometimes at school, Wade would put on sunglasses and walk right ahead of Darryl, making sure people didn't get too close to him as they walked down the hall. No one had ever noticed Darryl before, but now when they turned to see who this little dude with the sunglasses was keeping safe, they'd see Darryl and say, "Who's that?" and Wade would hurry Darryl along, so he never heard them say, "No, seriously, I have never seen that guy before." And sometimes he did subtle-to-the-point-of-almost-unnoticeable things, like when a brisk wind would blow in, as it often did, as Darryl was writing in his binder, as he often was, and Wade would position himself just so, and Darryl would nestle himself and his slightly ruffling binder pages unknowingly into the slipstream.

It was nice. Like those animal friendships — a rabbit that looks after a deer just because they met at the right time. Adorbs.

One time Darryl found Wade watching a video: "How to Whistle WHILE You Work!" He was struggling something fierce with making the sounds. His thin, dry lips were exactly the opposite of what the video said he needed. Darryl gave him the same advice his mother had given him when he'd tried this same thing: give up, since what use was whistling except to draw attention to yourself? Wade agreed. Later that year, he and Wade were hanging out at the mall food court, celebrating Darryl's birthday, when a thin, reedy whine started coming out of Darryl's nose — allergy season, and Darryl was allergic to most things. Everyone in the food court started looking around to find the poor creature that was making the horrible noise and put it out of its misery. Darryl's face went a deep red as he felt the crowd homing in on him. But then, beautiful, echoey birdsong filled the air. Everyone turned their attention to see where it was coming from. Darryl started looking too. It seemed to be coming from everywhere and nowhere, and so Darryl gave up. "So weird, right?" he said, his eyes settling back on Wade. Which was when he realized the ethereal sound was whistling, emanating from Wade's thin, dry, pursed lips. And Wade wasn't just whistling, he was . . . ventriloqwhistling. Wade raised his eyebrows in recognition and said — or rather, cheeped — to Darryl, "Happy b-day, dude."

Things were always superchill between him and Wade. For instance, they could sit in Wade's room for hours, still and quiet, and listen to Wade's records, and sometimes they could sit in Wade's room for hours, still and quiet, even when there wasn't any music playing.

Sure, many of their talks, when they weren't being still and quiet, consisted of "IKR, right?" But the thing was, they did know, and they were right.

Figure 5
Wade Was . . . Ventriloqwhistling.

Darryl, always uncomfortable with expressing his thoughts or fears, found himself trying to with Wade. Without Darryl really being conscious of it, Wade had built a buffer that made Darryl feel safe, a nice, cozy vacuum. With all that quiet just begging to be filled, he tried stuttering out some complaint about life or his family or school or this sense of inadequacy that had plagued him since sixth grade, and, no, maybe he wasn't able to actually give voice to the uncomfortable, unsettling complication of stuff roiling around inside him, but then he wouldn't need to. Darryl would start and stop and start and stop until, softly, gently,

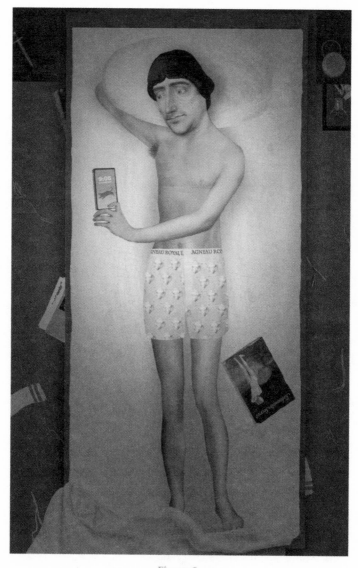

Figure 6
"He Knew He Shouldn't Look."

Wade would place his hand on Darryl's knee and say, "I know, right?"

But then one morning Wade's mom discovered Wade had died peacefully in his sleep while hanging from a rafter with a rope tied around his neck.

And that was rough.

Wade had been writing him a text the night he died, the three dots showing Wade was typing him a message were still shimmering like a mirage. And they were there for a few days, until finally Wade's parents turned his phone off.

In the bottom corner of the last page of Wade's section of the binder, Darryl added:

"..."

✺

In the quiet of his bedroom, he spent the morning playing connect the dots, tracing between the bumps and various misshapen moles that covered his body to see how many different figures he could make. It was a good game, Darryl thought.

Challenging, kept your mind sharp, and, best of all, played alone, even though Darryl often closed his eyes and imagined he was playing with someone else, as he was doing now. He was just about to break his record of forty-eight constellations when his phone buzzed.

He knew he shouldn't look. All summer long, Jude and Mary, who weren't friends per se, but weren't not friends either — "friends" is hard, Darryl thought — had been tagging him in photos of themselves enjoying their wicked-cool summer vacations.

He read through their latest batch of breezy updates.

Mary_M: Front row tickets at the Coliseum! #ReleaseThe Lions! #BestSummerEver #WhenInRome #HiDarryl #NoReally
JustJude: Resort vomitorium righteous! #IScreamJude ScreamsforIceCream

He wanted to share some pics of his own of the equally

wicked things he'd been up to, tell them about the new language he'd been working on, the great dreams he'd been having, how he'd learned some ankle-breaking b-ball moves, but he remembered his mother's advice: "An eye for an eye is just stupid, Darryl. Also what are you doing touching your face with your pink eye?"

Instead, he replied, *#DoingJustFineMyselfThanks ForAsking*, and then stared at the screen, his thumb hovering over "post," and his eyes blurred all of a sudden. He wiped them and his hand came away wet, and he realized they had just — somehow — filled with tears. He sighed and deleted his message.

Then he typed, *I want what you have*, but he deleted that even quicker, as if they could see, and typed, *Jelly!*, instead and pressed "send."

He opened up his binder to better catalog his feelings. He pulled a bit too hard on the ACHES & PAINS tab and accidentally opened a secret hollowed-out part where he had hidden a couple of fortune cookies. Not one to ignore coincidence, Darryl broke one open and read the beguiling message:

When a caterpillar thinks the world is over, it becomes a butterfly.

He thought about this for a minute. How it was that something that's almost perfectly invisible one day just makes a little shell around itself: "So long, everyone!" as if everyone were listening. Then after a sweet dramatic pause — boom! it's back! — miraculous, beautiful, the kind of thing people hope will wind up on their finger or, better yet, on a sweet poster in their first apartment. The kind of thing no one would confuse with the original, mostly forgettable thing. The kind of thing people are super-sad about when it dies. Metamorphosis was appealing, Darryl thought. But he knew this wasn't how the world worked. Like his dad always told him, "You're stuck with what you've got, Darryl — not

Figure 7
He Wanted to Share Some of the Equally
Wicked Things He'd Been Up To.

*

Figure 8
"He Was Surprised by How Very Low Her Opinion Was of Him."

✳

a lot! Ha ha!" Darryl resigned himself instead to a smaller change, like maybe Jude's nickname for him would catch on, and when people would pass him, they'd say, "Hey, Tray!" and Darryl would wave back, *Hey, yeah, that's me. Tray. Thanks for noticing.*

He bit into the cookie.

The cookie was stale.

🐾

Darryl pulled himself out of bed with a groan, as he often did. As if she'd been listening with her ear pressed against his door, his mom immediately hollered from the other side, "What are you doing in there? Get up, it's late!"

And while he was eating breakfast, she came up behind him and threw a stack of papyrs on the table. "How about you go get a job," she said. She tapped her finger on the pile. "I already filled these out. All you have to do is drop them off."

He had to admit, it was something to do, but still. He looked down into his bowl of ancient grains cereal, where he'd fashioned a little smiley face out of the floating chunks. As if on cue, the chunks sank away and Darryl's reflection was the only face left.

It wasn't that Darryl didn't want to get a job. And not that he didn't understand the power of a hard job well done, of hanging in there, of reaching for the top. He'd seen the motivational posters at school and that his mom put up in their living room, and above his bed, and he felt he understood them. He'd even spent a lot of time thinking about all the jobs he'd be excellent at — skateboard and/or chariot designer! junior assistant! silversmith who makes sick scarab pendants! producer! — but these kinds of gigs proved elusive to a guy whose only work experience was sweeping the sand off his neighbor's walk, and he'd only done that the one time to fulfill his school's volunteer requirement.

But looking at the jobs she'd thought he'd be good at, he was surprised by how very low her opinion was of him. Barista? No thanks. Short-order cook for Jude's dad's Kebab Hut? Gah. Pass. Night security at the olive garden? Hard pass.

What his mom didn't understand was, he was too ambitious for a job. A "job" would clip his wings. Foreclose on loftier possibilities. What was he going to do? Waste all his raw talent realizing someone else's life dream?

Still. If he had a job, something dangerous like piercing ears at the Piercing Pagoda, maybe then he'd meet a cool

girl. Better yet, a cool girl with a boy's name. Like Sam. Or Vinny. Or Charley. Or Wade.

A job would have added some variety to his summer, for sure. Four weeks in, Darryl was feeling as lonely as Gregory the Penitent, the local hermit who hadn't talked to anyone in twenty-six years. Or not quite as lonely, because everyone knew loneliness was Greg's passion, and you gotta respect someone so committed. Darryl knew that all cool people thrived on loneliness, but he was not feeling so cool.

"Early bird, go get that worm," his mom said, taking his breakfast away before he'd even finished. "Also, there's a sandstorm coming and I need you to pick up some things from the store when you're there dropping off your application." And she kicked him out.

�*/

Darryl stood in the middle of the Tofu Tent, the neighborhood's first and only health-food store. He'd dropped off the other applications, but most of the proprietors had looked him up and down and then stared at his jaunty beret as they told him they weren't actually hiring right now.

This wasn't exactly where he wanted to be on a Thursday afternoon in the middle of summer, and with a sandstorm on its way. He looked at his mother's shopping list. Grains, duh. Some unleavened bread (his mother believed yeast to be too stimulating at this point in Darryl's life), some anise (which they kept behind the counter and which Darryl decided he would not ask for, since no matter what he always mispronounced it), and "some yogurt," she wrote, "NOT the Greek kind," because his mother didn't love the Greeks or their yogurt, but did she have to write that down?

The night manager was already on shift, called in early when everyone else left because of the sandstorm warnings. He was sighing loudly and wrapping day-old

Figure 9
"Darryl Was Feeling as Lonely as Gregory
the Penitent."

＊

carob muffins and setting them into a basket. Some of them looked a little smushed, like someone had poked them in the middle.

The night manager looked rough, red-eyed and pasty-skinned. Darryl didn't remember his name, but what Darryl knew about the guy was this: he'd taken the job at the health-food store on a whim because of a girl who worked there. Darryl had noticed her, too, used to try to time his trips to the store around her schedule, so he couldn't really begrudge the guy for following the patchouli scent of her right down the bulk

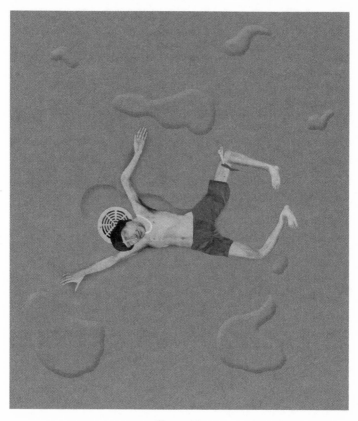

Figure 10
"Darryl Loved Sandstorms."

✴

aisle and applying for a job he probably didn't even want. But now, four years later, she was long gone — delivered to some other, better story, no doubt — and the night manager was still here, muttering about the customers who swoop in at any hint of a sandstorm and empty the shelves of everything.

"It's, like, one sandstorm, but now they come in here and buy farro for a month,"

he said. "Our next farro delivery doesn't come for another week and we're cleaned out, wiped out."

Farro was one of the grains Darryl's mom had sent him for, but Darryl wasn't going to mention that, and instead he scooped out a sackful of amaranth and a sack of freekeh for good measure. (Also, he couldn't resist an old-fashioned pelvic thrust any time he said the word "freekeh!" He wasn't sure why, but it felt right.)

"Is that all?" the night manager asked. "You don't want to buy sixty clay jars of water, just in case?" He motioned to the empty shelves behind Darryl. "Oh, never mind. We're sold out." He rolled his eyes.

Darryl noticed a handwritten sign taped to the shelves — HELP! — which he assumed meant employment, and he considered the crumpled, sweaty job application in his hand, and for a second, his head swam and his body swayed. He imagined himself in this guy's shoes, six or ten years from now, a horror show maybe, but better than nothing? But then his imagination went wild and he found himself in one of those surreal moments when it seemed to Darryl like he wasn't living his own life but was watching the lives of everyone else slip by him. He leaned hard into the checkout counter and tried to cover up his weird behavior by laughing too loudly at whatever the night manager was saying. But thankfully the night manager was distracted by the heaving winds outside, the violently ripping date trees. "Better get going if you don't want to get caught in the storm," he told Darryl. "Or else, I guess you could hang here till it passes if you want," he said, but Darryl didn't hear him, had already grabbed the grains and yogurt and run outside.

The wind ripped the application from his hands as soon as he opened the door. He

looked toward the horizon at the sandstorm speeding toward him, and he figured he should get home quick if he wanted to avoid it.

Not that he was afraid of sandstorms. Just the opposite. Darryl loved sandstorms. No, he really loved them. Loved the squeaky-crunchy feeling of sand in his teeth. The wind whisking away the smoke of the cigarettes he stole from his mom's purse. The way the sand blotted out the sun — usually so bright and so hot and beloved by happy people — and made it into a small, pale, charmless orb. Kind of like him, he thought.

He loved the way a sandstorm pubed up people's hair.

Plus, you never knew what the winds might blow in. When he was a kid, he would go out collecting after every sandstorm, hunting for shiny bits of metal cast about and polished to a sheen by the whipping winds and coarse grains of sand, or else the peppered squishy bits of desert rats not quite fast enough, caught up in the storm, torn to ribbons, and then dropped behind his house. (To be honest, he still did this after every sandstorm, but these days he just didn't tell anyone about it.) He wondered what this storm might bring — an ostrich leg? some micah? a fancy shoppe sign torn from its hinges in some far-off, exotic place and dropped right in his own backyard? SHELDON'S ACTUARIAL SERVICES — who knew!?

Also, he could cry in a sandstorm. Not just cry, but really weep, folding his heaving sobs into the wailing winds, and no one was the wiser. Yeah, sandstorms were the best.

But what he loved most of all about a sandstorm: they scared the crap out of Jude, who was so terrified of his hair being pubed up — mostly because sandstorms exposed the fact that his handsomely styled coif was actually just a very thin weave, sprayed in place, that would lift in the

Figure 11
"No, He Really Loved Them."

slightest breeze and reveal his majorly receding hairline — that he would forget, even briefly, his life's mission to torment Darryl.

Jude was now on vacation, but even still. Darryl was happy as he biked home, imagining Jude's terror-stricken face beneath his pubey 'do.

Darryl had known Jude since preschool. His first real memory of him, though, was from the time their second-grade class took a field trip to the local jail, part of an early "scared straight" program, and Jude tricked Darryl into stepping inside a jail cell ("The

doors only lock if you've done something bad"), and then locked Darryl inside, and then told on Darryl to their teacher.

The next day, before school, Jude gave Darryl a too-hard high five and said, "That was bitchin', man," and acted like they'd planned the whole thing together. And ever since, Darryl had been trying to come up with a word that might mean both an enemy and a friend, but so far all he could come up with was "enemeind," which, depending on how he pronounced it, sounded more like a cool foreign candy or like what his doctor always wanted to give him, and, in any case, it never sounded quite right.

They had some good times. Like that one night when Jude secretly filmed Darryl through his window enjoying some alone time and posted it on his socials for all his Roman bros (or #RoBros, as he called them) to make fun of. Or that other time in gym when they had to partner up and do laps, and as soon as they got to the far end, Jude shoved him onto the ground in the tall grass. Darryl thought that was kind of a dick move, but then Jude fell down beside him. They stayed there, out of sight from the teacher, whipping pebbles at the students running by who weren't nearly as brilliant as they were. That was kind of fun and funny. When he saw Jude's genuine delight every time a stone elicited a yelp, it dawned on Darryl that maybe cruelty was Jude's way of touching the world. Who was Darryl to judge? Besides, he enjoyed being on the blunt side of malice for once. When it came time to report to the teacher how many laps the other had done, Darryl lied and said Jude had done seventeen, which was pretty good. And when the teacher asked for Darryl's total, Jude said two, which was not as good.

Darryl didn't quite understand Jude, who seemed to mostly hang out with Romans and who once said, "It'd be so cool, right, to become a

Figure 12
"Darryl Was Happy as He Biked Home."

*

Centurion?" But whenever Darryl saw him with the Romans—usually hanging out on his roof throwing fistfuls of olives, the canned ones, down at his slaves or sometimes just at the people walking down the street—he never looked happy, but instead like he wanted so badly to be having a good time that at any moment, the stress of it would give him a heart attack or make his face explode. And he had no

Figure 13
Darryl Enjoyed Some Alone Time.

*

idea why Jude was even his friend, except one time Darryl said something — he couldn't even remember what — that made Jude laugh so hard he spit milk out his nose; and even though Jude gave Darryl a super-wicked charley horse for it, he kept coming around at lunchtime, standing around, drinking from cartons of milk, asking Darryl if he had any other hilarious jokes to share.

Well, and also because Jude wanted to be in Darryl's band.

Originally, Darryl's band — a bitchin' power duo called the Diffrents — featured himself on guitar and vocals and Mary on drums. And last summer, they

had finally found their groove. Originally-originally, the band had been just him, a solo act called Diffrent, and he imagined ending a concert in front of a throng of screaming fans by saying, "Thank you, Naz! I am Diffrent!" But then Mary had heard him practicing this, and when he opened his eyes after imagining bowing before his screaming fans, she was staring at him through his bedroom window, and he almost yelped. He smiled weakly and waved at Mary, who simply nodded back and walked off, and he figured she was on her way to tell everyone in the world what a freak he was. But then two seconds later, she knocked on his front door and told him, "We gotta find a place for my kit," and then gestured to the stack of drums on his front walk.

Darryl asked himself if maybe this was a way to garner a new friend and, in that exact moment, decided that it theoretically could be, but not with Mary. She was too aloof to be friends with anyone, he told himself, but really it was that Darryl couldn't imagine — even though that's really all he ever imagined — having a friend who was also a girl without his brain combining the two words and making him blush. So he thought of her as a mate. A *band*mate. That was as far as he was willing to go. Mary didn't seem to care either way.

If anyone asked (no one ever did), they would have described their music as "very serious." They practiced five times a week to prove how very serious they were. Which was what they were doing when Jude swanned in.

Darryl was intently focused on his fingers, ripping through one of his favorite songs, and when he looked up, a smile on his face, Jude was there, airguitaring like an idiot, and Darryl stopped smiling. Jude had a guitar strapped to his back, and he swung it around, slid it on the floor in front of him, and started playing it with his bare foot while

keeping time on the studio's ancient piano.

Darryl wanted to stop but Mary kept pounding the skins, so he played until the song ended.

"I figured we could use a keyboardist," Mary said. "So I invited Jude over. You guys are friends, right?"

Darryl felt betrayed but also like he needed his bandmate, and Mary wasn't entirely wrong about them being friends.

"Cool!" Darryl chirped.

Saying no is hard.

Jude soon took over as frontman and renamed the band Just Jude. Darryl got bumped to rhythm guitar. Sometimes he just pretended to play, silently strumming above the strings while Jude goofed off. Darryl could see that Jude enjoyed goofing off, had maybe never had an opportunity to really goof off before, at least not without one of his RoBros yelling "Goof!" at him, and meaning it in the cruel way and not the friendly way.

Plus, at least Darryl was part of something bigger now, and could tell anyone who asked, "Yeah, I'm in a band," although no one ever asked. Also, say what you want about Jude's never-ending keyboard solos, last summer was the opposite of forgettable.

This whole summer had been a bit less, well, distinct. Every sunrise, dialing up his well-rehearsed routine. Ancient grains for breakfast. Rolling around bored in his bedroom. Heavy sighs, which he theorized were good for his asthma. Soul-searching. Morning nap. Some quality alone time. By lunch, his mother kicked him out of the house. "Go find some friends already!" she'd say, oblivious to how impossible — and to his mind, unnecessary — this was. Besides, *she* was the one who had taught him that nothing good ever comes from leaving the house: "There's just trouble out there — it's not a good place to be." Anyway. Twenty minutes of the

Figure 14
"Saying No Is Hard."

✻

not-so-great outdoors. Late-afternoon nap. Binder Blast time. And all day, posts from Mary and Jude reminding him of all the lives that were so very different (and dangerous and terrifying and schedule-disrupting, he noted) from his.

He easily added his standard thumbs-up emoji to Jude's posts, but Mary's were trickier. If he overthought it, as he was prone to doing, it was *kind* of like she was talking directly to him. He had never done any of the insane things depicted in her images — waterskiing out-of-bounds; tumbling down insanely tall sand dunes;

wearing sunglasses that weren't specifically protecting him from harsh UV rays — and had never been fun or flirty with anyone online before. And as a result his responses — "Nifty outfit!" "That looks dangerous! Take care of that body of yours!" — seemed like they were written by a creepy old man. Mary did him a solid and deleted his comments almost as soon as he posted them.

Even though he'd had better summers, the prospect of school starting up again in the fall loomed larger than usual. Not that school had ever been awesome. There was the constant threat of hummus being thrown at the back of his head at lunch, or spooned into his gym shoes, or smeared on his seat or his face. Not that anyone had actually done these things to him, but they could have, had they noticed him. It was strange, actually, since all this stuff seemed to have happened to Wade all the time. Anyway. Darryl found himself in the awkward position of wishing he'd be the target of bullying, since what better way to prove you existed?

He put himself out there a few times, even signing up for some extracurriculars, like Grades Over Girls, an after-school study club. When he arrived, snacks in one hand, calculator in the other, there were no girls, and no guys either. It turned out to be fake, one of Jude's hilarious pranks. It also turned out to be livestreamed. For a fleeting moment, people knew who he was — "that moron in the video" — but, like all memes, he was destined to be shunted out of the spotlight by the next morsel of bite-size hilarity.

But this year — senior year — could be different, right?

This was the year when students were belatedly taught "All About Your Changing Body," and Darryl still had quite a few questions about this written in his binder, so he was already way ahead of the game.

Figure 15
The Prospect of School Loomed Larger Than Usual.

It was also the first year he'd be without Wade.

Even though, based on past experience, school would be a blur of unmemorable events, without Wade, it was likely to be, well, different. Maybe filled with relentless daily humiliations? That might be an interesting change of pace. What's the worst that could happen? He'd spend the rest of his school career eating lunch at the lepers' table? They seemed friendly, and had great dark humor — like whenever someone shed a body part, they'd play hot potato, then freak out the RoBros by tossing it their way. And it was better than

Figure 16
This Was the Year Darryl Learned About His Changing Body.

*

being stuck at the social lepers' table, which even the teachers steered clear of.

He hung on to this thought as he imagined himself heading back, with a knapsack full of hope, an out-of-date phone, and the captain's hat and dress shoes his mom had found discounted in the "unisex" section. He was "all ready for the friendship to set sail," as she so jauntily put it.

He thought about what he would do after school was done for good. But not, like, just an after-school or summer job, but what was he going to do for a career? What was going to be his path forward in this life?

His local options were limited, since the town was often described in online reviews as "unbelievably rinky-dink" and "a real shithole," but he imagined them anyway. He could become a farmer, maybe. Plant olive trees, maintain a grove of olive trees. Not that he'd been any good at the sprouting projects in school, as he'd always killed his bean sprouts, but as a farmer, he'd get a great tan! Maybe an artisanal practice of some kind, like apprenticing at the tannery? Nipple-deep in dye, scraping the gristle off the hides of his favorite animals? Ditto on that tan, but he wasn't sure how happy he'd be tanning hides. Maybe if he worked hard enough slinging falafel at the Kebab Hut, he could learn enough about the quick-service food industry to open his own fry-stand. Sure, he might get severely burned, *but* maybe the skin grafts would replace some of his horrible skin!

Heavy odds had him working on the Roman road project, like his uncle and his cousins and his grandfather, who had keeled over on the job one hot afternoon, and they built the road right on top of him. Every time they drove over grandfather-speed-bump, his mother would sigh and say, "It's nice he could make a difference in people's lives." That *was* nice, Darryl thought.

All this thinking about the distant future was making him tired, and so Darryl focused his attention on the only true bright spot — seriously, just the one — coming up on the cultural calendar. The annual Flutes and Lutes Festival. Normally such a thing would be held in nearby Naz, but his town's distinctive features — all the flat empty land, the lax human-waste-disposal laws, the shifting sands that effortlessly buried anyone who decided to lie down outside for a bit — made it the perfect fit for the festival.

Watermelon Pie and the Eunuch Brothers were on the

Figure 17
"Heavy Odds Had Him Working on the Roman Road Project."

*

bill. He'd thought he'd *never* get to see them live in concert. He would buy a sausage on a stick and then maybe find a cool hacky-sack game to join. He'd jump into the mosh pit and prove himself so awesome at moshing he'd get some great friends and a different, less-cruel, more-cool nickname like Thrasher. Or Derrick.

That is, if he bought tickets. Which he hadn't yet. He had the money. He had nothing on his schedule that whole week. But buying

tickets would set a whole series of events in motion, all of which would bump him out of his lovely little rut. He could navigate his current life with his eyes closed, and there was something to be said for efficiency and ritual, a frictionless existence. An object in motion. If it ain't broke. Etc. He could do this forever, he thought.

Darryl stood alone in his front yard, the sand peppering his eyeballs, as he contemplated exactly how long forever was.

By the time he'd come to the conclusion that there was no conclusion, and he'd completely forgotten about getting tickets, the storm had been upgraded to a category-5, full-on haboob, Darryl's favorite.

He laughed as the wind tried so hard to carry him away, and it took a second for him to realize there was another sound coming through the howling.

Someone else's laughter?

A guitar?

Figure 18
The One Bright Spot on the Cultural Horizon.

‡

He thought he could smell incense, but not the brand his mother put in his basketball kicks to mask the odor; this was sweeter, less toxic smelling. Then, out of the swirling gloom, a broken-down cart appeared. It pulled up at the house next door, which had been empty for almost a year now. A man and a woman hopped off the cart, smiled brightly, so brightly he could see their teeth even through the driving sand, and gave him a friendly thumbs-up before they went inside.

Huh, Darryl thought. Happy refugees.

The woman stuck her head back out the door and called in an incredibly lovely, singsongy way, "Jaaay-aay!"

Darryl turned, following her voice back to the cart, his hope soaring. Please, please, please, let it be a girl with a guy's name.

A figure emerged from beneath a blanket. Through the fog of sand, the figure looked thin and tall and like she had blond hair, cut kind of jagged and cool. The sandstorm had delivered . . . But then a gust of wind knocked her hair—which was actually just straw—off the kid's head, and what was left was a brown-haired boy his age. Dorky but not dorky too. Different.

Jay.

He looked at Darryl and up-nodded. Darryl played it cool and turned away.

❧

As soon as he came inside, Darryl fetched his binder and drew a Venn diagram with three perfect circles, one labeled DARRYL, the other JAY, and the last one MEMORIES OF WADE.

It wasn't that Darryl didn't want any new friends, or that he didn't think friends were desirable, but so far all he'd really had to go on in the friends department was Jude, his enemiend, and no-longer-here Wade. He felt kind of ruined for friends at the moment. They were too risky. Or so he assumed. The Venn diagram would tell him anyway. Nothing beats the scientific method when it comes to friends, Darryl told himself, and as a matter of fact, they should call it a Friend diagram. Then he told himself, Maybe this is why you don't have any friends.

He looked at the diagram, saw that a sliver of overlap was indeed possible. He nodded sagely. He could become acquainted with this guy, Jay, but nothing more.

❧

Becoming acquainted with Jay meant finding some way to meet Jay.

Figure 19
A Boy His Age. Dorky. Different.

He tried the casual "hanging like a cool guy" thing where he stood in his empty front yard, squinting at the horizon like cool guys do, and hoped Jay might see him out there and, curious about what this cool guy with nothing to do was looking so intently at in the distance, come outside, too, and say, *Hello, what are you looking at? Do you want to do something?* He also tried the casual "walk in front of Jay's house as if on the way somewhere interesting" and the "walk back past Jay's house as if on the way home from somewhere interesting," with the thin hope Jay might see him

Figure 20
"It Was Actually Jay's Mother with Whom
Darryl First Acquainted Himself."

out his front window at just those moments, or maybe he would step through the front door himself, also on his way somewhere interesting and in need of a companion who would be cool with that.

Surprisingly, none of that worked.

It was actually Jay's mother with whom Darryl first acquainted himself, by watching her through her window while trimming and retrimming the hedge in his side yard until his mom yelled at him, "All right. That's enough of that, Darryl!"

As Darryl was putting away the hedge trimmers, Jay's mom came up to him and introduced herself. "Hello, my name is Mary. I think you're our new neighbors." She said other things, too, but he couldn't hear any of them; he could only stare at her. He couldn't help himself. Jay's mom was the most beautiful woman he'd ever seen, and it was as if a soft nimbus of light encircled her entire beautiful face, like she was standing in front of a late-afternoon sun. Except this happened even when there wasn't any sun, like at night even.

He must have smiled and nodded at something, because then Jay's mom smiled back at him and said, "Good. Jay will be so happy to hear that." And then she turned and was gone and he sat down on a barrel by the toolshed, his knobbly knees no longer able to hold him up.

He learned a lot while night trimming. Once he heard her tell Jay, "Look, there are going to be troubles — troubles are part of the deal, my friend."

Deal? What deal?

And friend? Could you be friends with your mother? All he got from his own mom was, "What do you do to these shoes to make them stink so bad?" But Jay's mother talked like a rabbi, confident and knowing.

Darryl found it incredibly stimulating.

Jay's dad was always in his woodshop, which was really just their back shed with its door open. He was a carpenter. Darryl never saw him working around town, only ever in the shed. Sometimes, Jay would hang out with his father while he worked, and they'd listen to music and drink tea, and when Jay got up to go, they'd hug, and his dad would say, casually as anything: "Love you, Jay. You going to that flutes concert?"

"Love you, too, Dad. Yeah, for sure, might be fun."

Darryl had never seen anything like it. The only time

Figure 21
"Jay's Dad Was Always in His Woodshop."

his own dad had "hugged" him was whenever he reached around him to grab something from the fridge.

Darryl couldn't figure out either of Jay's parents, who seemed nothing at all like his own.

But even still, they were nothing compared to Jay himself, whom Darryl watched from a safe distance while narrating the sequence to himself in hushed tones, as one does when observing a rare creature performing its everyday tasks in a miraculous new way: "Jay lay on the ground and stared at a single flower for the entire day — all

by himself, studying a single petal as if it contained some profound mystery that everyone else could see if they only knew how to look, but like really look."

Another time Darryl saw Jay standing on his parents' roof, eyes closed, face pointed to the sun, his arms outstretched, taking in the warmth and the light but also something else. It was like he was vibrating, as if all he wanted was to get closer to the sun, get closer to the sky and everything above it.

It was weird.

It hit Darryl: Jay knew nothing about him. He was pretty sure Jay wasn't creepily spying on his life. He didn't know if Darryl was good at chess, or really understood poetry, or was able to snap his fingers, didn't know that he'd failed miserably at each of these. If he were to become friends with Jay, Darryl could be anything he decided to be. A chance to reinvent himself, without all the hassle and dust-raising of moving to a new town.

Figure 22
He Stared at a Flower for the Entire Day.

⚹

Hm.

He pulled out his phone and navigated to the Flutes and Lutes Festival site. All the good seats were gone, since the concert was, well, the next day. So he selected general admission. Admit one. And then he clicked on the shopping cart. And then he checked out.

⚘

By the next day, Darryl had worked himself into a knot of anxiety he wasn't sure he could untangle. But not for nothing had he used fancy armpit lye and learned to whistle a few tunes, to clap without his hands aching so bad.

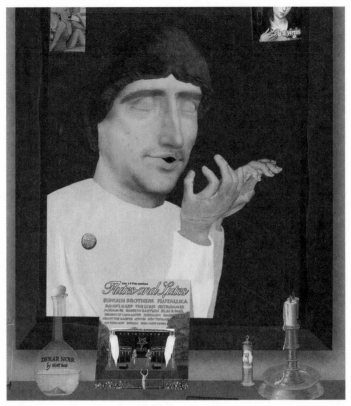

Figure 23
It Gave Him the Squirt of Adrenaline He Needed.

*

Sorting out these myriad accomplishments gave him the squirt of adrenaline he needed. He put his fancy beret — the one with the silk lining — in his pocket in case the urge to put it on came over him and left the house.

❧

The stands were full. A spillover crowd filled the square. The heat was melting Darryl's acne concealer. Darryl walked through the crowd while the first band set up. He casually hovered on the edge of

conversations, looking at whoever was speaking and nodding his head in agreement or chuckling at jokes, as if he were part of the actual conversation; sometimes he added clever rejoinders, then when the people turned to see who had said something to them, he turned, too, joining their search for the source of this wit, adding, "Ha ha, good one!"

Jay was nowhere to be found. Oh well, Darryl had tried. He settled in.

The opening act, Watermelon Pie, came out and played their only hit song, "Watermelon Pie," twice in the same set. Not incredible, Darryl thought, but it was a pretty good song, probably better than their new material.

There was a long break while Watermelon Pie broke down their equipment, during which Darryl fell deeply in love with a mysterious girl with blue hair. She looked right at him, and she smiled. Or rather, she was looking at something and smiling, and Darryl maneuvered himself in front of her gaze. Her expression changed to one of disgust, but Darryl was pretty sure that was because of the smell wafting from the portable toilets. She walked over to the food truck lines, and he followed her, but not like a creepy stalker or anything. Just. Like. Maybe she would stand in line and he could stand in line behind her and when she got to the front of the line and ordered her sausage on a stick, she'd realize she didn't have enough money, and she would smile shyly at him, and he would say something smooth, like... Well. He hadn't thought of anything smooth to say yet, but he would by the time she got to the front of the line, he was sure.

As he contemplated this delusion, the MC came out and walked to the mic.

"Rest of the show's canceled," he said. Everyone went quiet. "The band died of starvation on their way here. Sorry. No refunds."

Figure 24
Watermelon Pie Played Their Only Hit Song. Twice.

This news was not well received.

The crowd went insane.

In the middle of all the fighting and screaming and shoving and murdering, a figure stood up and looked peacefully at all the chaos around him.

Jay?

Jay was the last person in the world Darryl thought he'd see in the middle of a crowd. He seemed more like a lone wolf, the kind of guy who would only circle the fringes of a melée. He was kind of meta that way. But there he was, calm as a stone, in the very

Figure 25
"This News Was Not Well Received."

middle of this one. He stood up, and he looked peacefully at the chaos around him. And then . . . he pulled out a lighter and lit a flame and held it high up in the air, and one by one, people stopped. They stopped their fighting and gnashing and burning, and they looked at the flickering light.

And they calmed.
But not just the people.
The birds in the trees.
The shimmering heat.
The melée dust.
The wind and the rustling palm leaves.
The very earth seemed to settle into itself, as if it had let out a long-held, tense breath.

Figure 26
"The Crowd Went Insane."

*

It was the coolest thing Darryl had ever seen.

Everything changed after that. People gathered in orderly lines and returned to their homes in a respectful but weirded-out silence, like kids heading back to a day care after a day in the park, as if they couldn't help themselves, as if some unseen force tugged at their sleeves or moved their feet in a slow but steady shuffle.

Darryl was awestruck. He followed Jay at a distance, scuttling between parked carts. Finally, Jay stopped, turned, and said, "Um. I can see you, you know. You're *right* there."

Darryl poked his head up. Jay beckoned Darryl over.

The two had never spoken a word to each other.

They didn't stop talking the entire way home.

※

Summer with Jay was a total revelation, and unlike any summer Darryl had experienced in his entire life. Whatever they did felt charmed. They got up to stuff their parents would never have approved of, like giving Darryl's Kebab Hut uniform to the weird old guy who lived in a dumpster behind the restaurant and persuading him to take Darryl's shifts. They pretended to argue in sign language in front of strangers, one time Jay getting so excited by their fake fight, he flipped over a table at the farmer's market and sent tomatoes and squash and money scattering everywhere. They made it a rule to sprint away every time they saw Roman mall cops, daring the cops to chase after them, and even though they never did, they totally could have. Darryl took him to his favorite sandstorm spot, and Jay seemed to really enjoy it; he had this way of holding his hand, pointed to the sky, like he was throwing a gang sign, and the sand just swirled over and around him, leaving him clean as a whistle. They invented supercool, unnecessarily complicated handshakes — any excuse, really, for lingering contact.

Darryl was feeling something he couldn't quite get a handle on or name. Joy, maybe? Impending doom?

Kind of, but no. None of those, exactly.

Then he hit upon it.

Pressure. That's what he felt. The pressure that came with having something to lose. Someone to lose.

※

One day they found a tall sycamore tree sprouting leaves bigger than their faces, and as if on a dare, they climbed into it, higher and higher into its canopy, and, just when Darryl

Figure 27
"Summer with Jay Was a Total Revelation."

*

thought they'd climbed high enough or maybe even too high (he'd never climbed a tree before, fearing for the brittle bones his mother had warned him he'd inherited), Jay winked and gave him a smile and climbed even higher, and Darryl followed. By the time they reached their destination, high enough that the breeze was fresh and you could see beyond the town limits, marked by the road that encircled and encouraged people to bypass the town entirely, his bones had never felt less shatterable.

The tree became their hideout, their safe space, their

Figure 28
"Any Excuse, Really, for Lingering Contact."

circle of trust. Protected by its oversize leaves, they revealed secrets they could never have spoken out loud on the ground. Darryl told Jay about his dreams of becoming a producer or a junior executive assistant, he told Jay about how nervous Mary made him sometimes, with her small, dark eyes, and how pink the very tips of her hair were, and how, sometimes, when she wore a certain T-shirt and she was really wailing on her drums, her arms would rise high over her head to bash away at the cymbals before coming down hard on the snare or the toms, and he would see a flash of

pale, soft-looking skin in the middle part of her body, and how sometimes he secretly adjusted the cymbals a bit higher.

But mostly, his stories involved his fears, or more often, his "condition."

Red eyes, tingling fingertips, skin so sensitive even his hair hurt. He was certain these symptoms were signs of (he mouthed the word) . . . *leprosy*.

Jay always listened, with no judgy face, ever. He promised never, ever to tell, and better yet? He didn't change the way he acted around Darryl, not even after the (he whispered the word inside his head) . . . *leprosy* stuff came out, didn't flinch or pull away if Darryl accidentally-on-purpose brushed up against him. He didn't make excuses as to why he couldn't hang out or had to go home early. Darryl remembered reading once that you should ask your sad friend about the sad thing they never talk about, and though Jay never did, Darryl felt that

if he had, he could tell him, *would* tell him, since Darryl had shared his most shameful fears, and Jay hadn't blinked. He didn't tell Jay about his binder, since, well. But he thought he might. Someday.

They named their tree Rooty but pronounced it "Wooty." The kind of thing that kids do when they are still sort of kids.

※

Jay told his own stories, of course, but Jay's stories were, well. Different.

Most of them sounded too crazy to be true. Like that time his parents woke him in the middle of the night and told him they had to leave, right now, but never told him why or where they were going or what was chasing them away. Or how Jay got braces, and the next day, the braces just fell off and his teeth were perfect, and he never had to wear headgear for six years like Darryl did. Or that one time he was by a silty stream and gathered some water and made it

Figure 29
The Tree Became Their Safe Space.

*

pure and clean ("How?" Darryl had asked. "I don't know," Jay had said. "I just did.") and then with some clay formed sparrows — twelve of them — that then flew away.

"They always fly away," he said with almost a sigh.

But, really, everything about Jay was different.

Also he had two dads.

"A stepdad?" Darryl asked.

"No," Jay said.

"A gay dad?"

"No."

"A sperm-donor dad?"

Jay thought about this. "Sort of, I guess," he said.

❧

One day in the tree, Darryl started speaking like he'd swallowed helium. He'd been practicing this voice in his room for quite a while now, but never once thought he'd use it in front of an actual living person, and never ever in front of someone as sublime as Jay. Except, here it was, out in the world, hanging in the air between the two of them, like some embarrassing gas he wished he could suck right back in.

That's that, Darryl thought. It's over. He would be able to write extensively about this moment in just about every section of his binder: HUMILIATION. SHAME. WRETCHED NEWS.

Darryl didn't know what to do.

The thing was, Darryl didn't trust trust, didn't really understand the vulnerability at the center of true friendship, not since that game of truth or dare he'd played with Mary and Jude, when Darryl shared that his dad still only made minimum wage — "Crazy, right?" — and within days, everyone at school was calling him "Tray," short for "Trailer Trash." "Sorry . . . but at least you have a nickname now?" Jude said. And that was true.

Jude did not have a nickname — except the one his family's slaves used behind his back, which wasn't even really a name; it was just a long string of really bad words. Even his

Figure 30
He Took L'il Wade Under His
Wind.

full name, Jude Jr., after his father, meant he didn't have his own real name either. Even though Darryl had spent his whole life trying to be both invisible and forgettable, this struck him as kind of heartbreaking, and made Darryl wonder if what Jude had only ever really wanted in this world was for someone to like him enough to give him a nickname. Except when he tried to give him one—Darryl went in soft, with a singsongy "Hey . . . Dude!"—Jude said, laughing, "Remember in third grade when I called you 'Tray' that one time and for, like, the whole year? Awesome."

In any case, nothing since Wade's death had convinced him that having best friends was how things were going to work out for him. His closest confidant since Wade was L'il Wade, a scorpion he'd found injured on the side of the road and taken under his wing, which he soon found out was an ill-advised place to put him. In fact, Darryl kind of still thought of big Wade as his closest pal. He'd taken great comfort in the fact that when Wade had died, he'd still been Darryl's best friend, so, in theory, they were still BFFs, or, as Darryl preferred, BFFEs. Forever and ever. And nothing could ever change that.

But then something miraculous happened: Jay used the voice, too.

They created a character for the voice, named "Mickey," and ever afterward took turns pretending to be him. As Mickey, they'd make goofy jokes, sure, but also, as Mickey, they'd tell each other awkward truths. Float tender and risky

compliments. Once, hanging out at Darryl's house, Jay told Darryl, "Mickey's cool."

And he *was* cool. It was all cool.

❧

Jay had to go into Naz with his dad, something to do with his dad's carpentry work. With Jay gone, Darryl felt a little at sea, loafing around so much that his mother finally locked him out of the house. He hid outside his bedroom window, where he could still get Wi-Fi on his phone, and was deep into *Pestilence Excellence!* — a video medley of the year's top ten plagues — when his mother changed the Wi-Fi password, casting him completely adrift.

Out in his front yard, he found himself edging closer and closer to Jay's house, maybe just to check to make sure that Jay wasn't home, or that he hadn't come back yet, even though it was still morning and Jay had been gone for only fifty-eight minutes or so. Without realizing what he was doing, he stood at Jay's bedroom window, and stared inside, imagining the two of them in there, goofing off and having fun, when, from behind him, Jay's mother said, "Hello, Darryl," so sweetly and with such gentleness in her voice, Darryl almost wept.

He turned and stammered out, "I'm — I'm sorry, I just."

But Jay's mother smiled. "I miss him, too," she said. "Funny, isn't it, how I saw him only fifty-eight minutes ago, and I already miss him." She smiled, and Darryl found his eyes welling up but also his mind filling with confusion. Adults didn't usually talk to Darryl like that. Adults didn't usually talk to Darryl at all. "But don't worry," she continued. "He'll be back soon."

Darryl hadn't been this close to Jay's mom by himself since that first time right after they moved in, and he felt mesmerized by her face, which looked gauzy, like the women in the movies his dad used to watch by himself late at night; but also, he thought he heard

Figure 31
He Was Deep into *Pestilence Excellence!* — a Video Medley of the Year's
Top Ten Plagues.

music, soft but majestic but also sad. She smelled terrific.

"He's very fond of you, Darryl," she said.

"I'm fond of him . . . too?"

"He needs you," she said. "He will always need friends like you, Darryl."

Darryl knew that was just Jay's mom being a mom, and that if Jay were there, he would smirk and roll his eyes at this sort of attention, but also hearing her say this made Darryl's chest expand so much, he thought it would explode.

"He's a special boy," she said, "and I'm glad he's found someone so special as a friend." She of course meant "special" in the nice way, not in the way his dad used it sometimes.

Figure 32
"A Bit of Light Tweezing Was All He'd
Need and He Would Be Golden."

*

Only later that night, when Darryl was in bed replaying this moment in his mind in slow motion, did he notice the strange look on Jay's mom's face when she said Jay was special. Jay was special, any dummy could see that. But when she said it, the look on her face made you think she was sorry for Jay, and was unhappy about how cool and special he was.

He closed his eyes and fell asleep, his mind trying hard to work out just where that music he heard had come from.

The weeks flew by. There weren't many ways Darryl didn't feel like a different person, but now, when he filled out *Good Girls* magazine's "R U So 😄😄😄 U Could ⚠ a 🔦?" questionnaire, he scored a solid 6 out of 10. Last time, even lying on his answers, he'd barely cracked 3 out of 10.

He lay back on his bed and stared up at the ceiling and thought about Jay and all they'd done together and realized that Jay hadn't just made him feel happier. He'd made him feel better. All his "symptoms" had subsided, the red eyes, the tingling fingertips. A thorough spelunking had produced a mostly clean bill of health. A bit of light tweezing was all he'd need and he would be golden.

He flipped open his tweezer satchel and grabbed his best pair and was just getting down to business when he heard a strange, unsettling noise.

It seemed to be coming from Jay's house.

He crept up to Jay's window. At first Darryl thought maybe Jay was playing some new experimental music, or that his family had adopted a hundred wild cats and set them loose in Jay's bedroom.

Then his mind spiraled into the idea that maybe he had other friends over — for a sleepover, or maybe he'd decided to start his own band — and Jay hadn't invited him . . . But all the lights were on in Jay's room, and Jay was the only person there, and there were no cats at all. It was just Jay, and he was . . . freaking out.

Eyes closed.

Thrashing about on the bed.

Moaning. Wailing. Screeching. Whimpering.

Weeping.

Darryl knew he should turn away. He knew he should go home. He knew this but he did not.

Whatever was happening to Jay, Darryl could feel it inside

himself, as if the sound were traveling into the earth, all the way to the center of the earth, and then back up through Darryl's toes and feet and legs, making its way through his special parts, then poking him, finally, in the back of his brain.

It made his whole world vibrate.

Darryl's left eye started twitching uncontrollably. And by the time Darryl got it under control, he realized Jay was looking right at him, wide-eyed and full of too many emotions and feelings for Darryl to comprehend. Which was when Darryl realized he was screaming, too. Or not screaming. Or yes, screaming, but also. Harmonizing.

He turned and ran.

⁂

Darryl didn't know what to do once he was back in his own room. Whenever he found himself with no good answer to anything—and nothing really to write in his binder— Darryl sometimes looked for answers on Wade's online memorial page.

The last post had been his own, and he refreshed the page just in case someone else had posted since he'd logged on. When he first came to Wade's page, he had been looking for someone who might've had insight into why Wade was gone. The page was full of comments, but not the kind he'd been hoping for, more along the weepy-mother kind, or the "Dude, that sux :(" sort. There were some that helped explain things that had always been a mystery to Darryl, like, "Sorry for punching U that time I meant to punch darryl but u got in the way," and "i didnt mean to put so much hummus in your shoes i thought those were your friends shoes?" And Darryl realized that Wade had done things for him, and he hadn't even noticed this. And this made him feel guilty. He added his own comment—#28 out of 45. It was succinct and, he thought, pretty profound:

Figure 33
"It Made His Whole World Vibrate."

*

"WTF?" Except, after, he realized it might not read the way he had intended it, and so he wrote a much longer entry explaining that he hadn't meant to be disrespectful with such a short comment. Over time, Darryl filled the wall with more comments and questions, interwoven with comments from others, "Youll be missed man but well party like u always wanted us 2!" and a lot of sad-face emojis, but not even the full-color emoji, just the :(version, so it looked even cheaper. Darryl felt it was his duty to overwhelm these comments with a shock-and-awe approach.

Finally, he typed out what he thought might be his last post to Wade: "I wish I knew what you knew." And then he fell into a very fitful sleep.

The next day, he and Jay were supposed to hang out, walk over to Rooty together one last time before school started up for real, but Darryl didn't know what he was going to do or say, or if Jay was even going to show up. He waited outside and the sun moved slowly across the sky and just when he was about to give up, the door to Jay's house opened, and Jay's mother stepped out and smiled her very special smile at Darryl, and then, before Darryl could settle his face into an expression of appropriate sadness and understanding, out stepped Jay.

Jay's mother stepped inside and closed the door behind her. Darryl nodded. Jay nodded back. They started walking in silence. And then:

"Mickey's sorry you saw that."

"Mickey's sorry, too."

"Oh, Mickey."

"Oh, Mickey."

FALL

ten hungry

ks revenge

ım

Paul – Here I sit, broken–
hearted, paid a dime and only...

Jay – Most likely to
be liked

Jim – Most likely to
become a 'GIF artist'

Sarah – Most likely to
inherit the earth.

Leah - Picture Not
Available

Darryl – Jay's Friend

Jude – Most likely to
think of himself.

Balthazar Jr.
aka 'Puke King'

Mary – "I will cut you."

Darryl slept through his alarm clock and had to run to school. He arrived sweat-stained (of course) and an hour late (naturally).

He stood outside homeroom and tried to peek through the door to catch the attention of Jude or Mary. Maybe they could distract the homeroom teacher enough for Darryl to sneak into class? Pretend he'd been there all along?

Not that he didn't have his fair share of anxieties, but one of Darryl's biggest was being called out by his teacher in homeroom for being late. Or being called out by his teacher in homeroom for anything at all, or being called out by anyone in any room, actually. Darryl had always felt most comfortable flying under the radar, which was why he shied away from being noticed and lived a life free from superlatives, always remembering the one nugget of advice his father had tossed his way: The tallest blade of grass is the first cut by the scythe, he'd said. So stay out of sight, Darryl.

But lately, he'd begun to feel something inside of him change, and as much as he usually wanted the world to pass him by, today he very much wanted Mary and Jude to notice him.

See, the two of them had been back from vacation for a few weeks now, he knew — he once saw the tail-end of Jude's tunic as he snuck out the back door of his dad's Kebab Hut; and when he was buying more farro for his mom at the health food store, he heard Mary's braying, hiccuping laugh, but then when he searched the aisles for her, he couldn't find her, and then he saw her through the front window, walking down the dirt road with another girl from school. She waved at him, but Darryl ducked out of the way as soon as she did. She had actually sent him a whole series of texts asking him how he was doing, but since he wasn't sure how to answer without

Figure 34
"He Arrived Sweat-Stained (of Course)."

professing something, he just deleted them.

He wanted them to look at him — and it was only them, certainly, and no one else — because he felt like he'd changed so very much, and he wanted them to look at him in a way that confirmed this for him.

He wished Jay was here with him; he'd know what to do with these feelings. Jay was great with conundrums, after all.

As he leaned closer to the door, he heard cheers coming from inside the classroom. Not just cheers but also a familiar voice. Jay! Darryl had

Figure 35
He Was Leading the Group in an Icebreaker of His Own Invention.

*

assumed Jay was one of those homeschooled kids who spent their days at the kitchen table reading civics pamphlets and watching things ferment. He imagined Jay's mom would be an excellent, amazing teacher. So patient. And amazing. Darryl had assumed he'd be the one to help Jay figure out how high school worked, if ever he wanted to take a break from his mom's home-schooling. And here he was, in Darryl's class, already the coolest classmate without any help from him, leading the group in an engaging icebreaker of his own invention. Something he called two truths and a lie.

Darryl opened the door and Jay raised his voice and gesticulated a bit more exuberantly so that Darryl could slide in without anyone noticing him.

Jay smiled and said, "I don't know, Mr. Whitaker, I think skydiving was the lie," before he sauntered over to Darryl and gently pulled him into the group. Darryl smiled weakly and then slipped into a desk at the back. Mr. Whitaker finally decided it was time to start class, and Jay took the seat beside Darryl.

Jay offered his hand, and they performed Darryl's favorite: palm up, palm down, down low, up high, flutter fingers.

At lunchtime, Darryl steeled himself for that first visit to the cafeteria, a place that had always magnified his wish to be both visible and invisible at the same time. Every year, it seemed, the first visit to the cafeteria had been a disaster. In the third grade, his belt loop caught on the doorjamb somehow and he ripped his pants all the way down the seam. In eighth grade, he left his new retainer on his food tray and spent the rest of the day crawling through the dumpster full of cafeteria mess trying to find it again. Last year, he dropped his fork on his way to the table, and when he bent down to pick it up, his backpack—slung over just one arm like everyone else's—swung round and knocked his whole tray onto the floor, and everyone clapped, and someone—Jude, maybe?—yelled, "Smooth move, Ex-Lax!" and everyone laughed. Including Darryl, because that was better, wasn't it, than crouching there in humiliated silence, or them finding out he had actually taken some of his mom's homemade Ex-Lax that very morning?

But as he and Jay made their way, something new happened. Jay extended his hands and the crowd parted, right down the middle. And as they walked—it seemed to Darryl like they were

Figure 36
"Something New Happened."

✳

floating — toward Mary and Jude's table, a couple of girls blushed. Some boys did, too. Darryl felt like he was in a scene from a movie, everything in slo-mo, backlit and glinting and cool.

"Who's your new friend, Daniel?" Murray, one of the blushing boys, asked Darryl.

"Oh, um," Darryl said. "This is Jay."

They slid onto the bench at Mary and Jude's table, and before they even got settled, Darryl, unable to contain himself, started unspooling their amazing tales of summer. Everyone listened, which was strange enough

Figure 37
"With Jay Around, Everything Was Just Better."

⁂

already, because usually whenever Darryl started talking, everyone disappeared. But everyone was still here. Not only that, but soon a crowd of kids surrounded him, listening, keen at first, and then... something else. Something new. Something different. At first, Darryl couldn't suss out what that something different was, since it was a feeling he'd only ever been on the dark side of, but after a minute he understood: it was envy.

❧

With Jay around, everything was just better. Popular girls acted smart-smart around Darryl, instead of mean-smart.

Bullies put him in a headlock, but only to give him friendly tickles. Almost no one pretended his skin was infected or disfigured, like the one year—last year, in fact—when the entire school acted like they couldn't touch him or else they'd become infected, too, and die. Crazy kids.

All because of Jay, Darryl knew. Just like he knew Jay could have ditched him at any moment and still have been friends with every other person at school, which was what Darryl had half expected Jay to do. But no, miraculously, his summer buddy stuck by him.

Not that everybody liked Jay. For whatever reason, Jude seemed to hate him.

Anytime Jay did something radically but subtly cool, like that time he made a perfect pass to some wallflower kid for a tap-in goal, or that other time he tore an apple into twelve perfect little boats to share, or when he brought a basket of fries to their table and the pile never seemed to go down, even though they were totally pigging out, Jude just rolled his eyes and muttered, "Dick."

Even when Jay offered some pointed social commentary, like when they walked by Throwback Thursday, the popular public stoning, and Jay told the guy running the thing, "Not cool," and the guy agreed it was indeed not cool and promised not to do it again, Jude said bitterly under his breath, "Moron."

This one time, a crowd of kids had gathered around Jay, who was sitting on the edge of the cafeteria stage and was telling some story about a manager? who was being dishonest? Darryl came in late, missed the beginning, but to be honest, sometimes even when he came in at the beginning of one of Jay's stories, Darryl found himself losing the thread of what he was talking about, mostly because he became mesmerized by the simple rise and fall of Jay's voice, which made him

Figure 38
"Jay Told the Guy Running the Thing,
'Not Cool.'"

*

feel calm and collected and uninterested in linear narrative. Anyway, this one time, everyone had gathered around, and as Darryl joined the crowd, he saw Jude standing on the perimeter, shaking his head. Then he tapped Mary on the shoulder and said, "Come on, I'm tired of this BS," but Mary shrugged him off and left Jude scowling and on his own. He turned and left, rolling his eyes at Darryl. "Nice work" — and here he hesitated, but just for a second — "dummy, bringing this one to school with you," Jude said, as if Darryl were

Figure 39
The Studio That Jude's Dad's Slaves Built.

responsible for Jay's entire existence. As if. As if!

All of which made Darryl wonder. But then he was interrupted while trying to make sense of this senselessness by a text from, speak of the Devil, Jude himself: *wrote a new song, binches! jam friday — the band is back!*

The band practiced at a nearby studio built by Jude's dad's slaves, which Jude brought up, like, all the time. "The slaves soundproofed the studio just last week," and, "Check out the detail on this carved molding. This one little slave dude did most of that. It depicts

all the key stages of them building the studio, including when they accidentally encased that little slave dude in the wall—insane!"

Once, Darryl overheard Jude arguing with his dad on their daily speakerphone call, and his dad said, "Why can't you be more like our slaves? At least they get shit done," which maybe explained Jude's obsession with the slave thing, though Darryl wasn't sure exactly how.

Darryl and Jay poked their heads in just as Jude plugged his mic into an amp. Jude was clearly not pleased to see Jay. He widened his stance at the mic stand and puffed up his chest and said through the amp, "It's pretty tight in here already?" Darryl had spent the morning convincing Jay to come to practice, mostly because he'd been talking up the band since the Flutes and Lutes Festival and the magic wasn't quite the same when he did solo performances for Jay in his bedroom. And now

he felt bad at this reception. "Also, not to mention?" Jude continued. "Studio sessions are kind of closed to the public?"

Jude's mother, who'd been tidying up nearby, marched over and grabbed Jude by the waistband of his underpants and whisked him around the corner. Mary shrugged and adjusted her cymbals, which were way too high again. Jay and Darryl looked at each other and waited. And when Jude returned a few moments later, he seemed smaller. Grudgingly, he made room for Jay—"But steer clear of the cords, man. It took the slaves all morning to lay those out"—and passed around the tab for his new song, "Killer! Summer!," along with some killer raisin muffins his mom had made.

Darryl and Mary felt their way through the opening bars. It wasn't super-complicated, but a couple of the chord changes felt weird. An augmented D7. A flatted fifth.

Then Jude started to sing. He sounded not terrible, actually. Most of the time, he sang with his eyes closed and this tortured look on his face, but this time, he opened his eyes back up and bugged them out at Darryl and Mary because they were about to miss their cue.

Darryl and Mary joined just in time, and it sounded even cooler.

But not quite cool enough. Not for Jude, anyway, who stopped singing and stepped back from the mic, chopping his hands through the air and yelling, "Cut, cut, cut, cut!"

Mary muttered just loud enough for Darryl to hear, "'Cut' is for movies, I think."

"That's not it, that's not it," Jude said, and for a second it sounded to Darryl like he'd affected some kind of accent, like British or Scandinavian?

"Sounded pretty cool to me," Jay said.

Jude glared at him and then spun on Darryl and Mary, shouting at them, "You sound like you're in choir. A school choir. Rough it up, man. You're using your mouse voice. I. Don't. Want. Mouse. Voice. I. Want. Lion. Voice!" Darryl shouted back, "Holy crap, dude, what?"

"Raw!" Jude yelled. "Epic! Totally destroyed! Is that too much to ask?!"

Darryl looked at Jay, who was wide-eyed at Jude's rant, and, it seemed, about to bail. And then something clicked in Darryl.

"Oh, oh, oh," Darryl said, because sometimes when he hit upon an epic idea, his brain and his mouth got tangled up in a loop. "Oh, oh, oh . . ." he continued. Then he stopped and pointed. At Jay. "You."

Jay looked surprised and said, "Am I ruining the vibe? I'm ruining the vibe. I'll go."

"Yeah, go," Jude said.

Darryl leaned forward and whispered to Jay, "You sing."

"Who sings? Wait. What?" Jude said.

"Me? No. I don't sing," Jay whispered back to Darryl.

"No, no, no," Darryl said. "Not singing. This is . . ." He paused. "That thing you do? At night? Sometimes?"

"Gross," Jude said. Mary nodded in agreement.

Jay's expression changed, darkened. He shook his head. *No way.*

"It'll be perfect," Darryl said. For whatever reason, convincing Jay to stand at the mic and wail seemed to be the most urgent desire he'd ever felt.

Darryl and Jay stared at each other for what seemed like an eternity, the conversation they were having with their eyes so all-consuming that Darryl didn't even hear Jude ranting about why no one else was allowed to sing his new song, until Jay stood up and Darryl wasn't sure if he was standing up to sing or to walk out, possibly forever.

Mary said, "We playing or what?"

Jay shook his head no again, but he seemed more resigned now.

"That's right. No way," Jude said. "No fricking way."

But Mary's sticks were already clacking together, and Darryl leaned his microphone over so Jay could reach it and hit his first chords, and Jude, unwilling to be sidelined, snarled into his mic, and Darryl and Mary joined in. After things got moving, Jay started singing.

Quietly at first. Stealthily. Like he was standing at the edge of a large, flat, still lake, so still it was like a mirror, and he knew if he dipped his toe in there he'd change it — maybe make it better, maybe worse, but no matter what, he'd make it different.

This hesitation didn't last long though — how could it? Once the wailing took off, there was no holding it back. And soon Jay's voice, rough as sackcloth, with a tortured vibrato to it, filled the room, and one by one the others fell silent.

Darryl's eye twitched. He knew this sound, of course,

Figure 40
He Knew This Sound. It Was What He Was Hoping For.
But Not Like This.

recognized it immediately. It was what he was hoping for, but he never imagined it would be like this. In the studio, with other people besides him listening to it, Jay's voice became something else, became everything else. Darryl's thoughts and fears and shames and humiliations, but the joys, too, fleeting though they might be, all of it rolled into one sound. And it destroyed him. It destroyed all three of them.

Darryl recovered first, and he goofed off on his guitar in an attempt to honor Jay's

Figure 41
They Had Invented Fire, and Now
Wanted Something to Burn.

intensity. The others followed suit, not wanting to be left out.

The song ended the way you run out of money: slowly and then all at once.

When they were done, when even the reverb and echo of the last note had finally dissipated, the four of them, winded and scooped out by it all, collapsed, even Jay, whose tunic was sweat-drenched and plastered to his chest.

Jude crawled over to Jay and seized him like a life preserver, more possessive than friendly, and said, through clenched teeth: "A singer is born!"

Figure 42
It Was a Catalog of the Things His Mother
Had Warned Him Against.

✶

It was dusk when they finally emerged from the studio, the rawest parts of themselves transformed into music. They stumbled outside, full to bursting with swagger.

They had just invented fire, and now they wanted — no, *needed* — something to burn.

So Mary set a trash can on literal fire, which is harder to do and grosser than you'd think.

Darryl tried his hand at reckless abandon. But quietly, where no one could see him and no one would get hurt.

Jude strutted.

Of course.

Jay pulled a sack of bowling balls out of nowhere, and together they rolled them down steep hills, cheering the sound of unseen crashes that drifted up out of the dark.

They made their way to downtown Naz, a place none of them had ever been.

Darryl felt like he was strolling through a catalog of all the dangerous things his mother had warned him against: lepers, thieves, fried pork, hunchbacks, women named after candy.

The stench of garbage juice, vomit, and frankincense aftershave hung thick in the air.

Haunted-house shrieks issued from an abandoned tenement as they passed it. Darryl shrieked back. The shrieks shrieked even louder, and Darryl about jumped out of his sandals.

Jay reached over and put a hand of bro-like calm on Darryl's shoulder, while with the other hand he casually high-fived some dude, vaped out of his mind, who was arranging a pile of trash in alphabetical order.

In that moment, Darryl felt almost unkillable.

�incomplete

They discovered the Sound Sack, a store overflowing with "different" music: braying donkeys and rhythm guitar, groaning slaves and whip-crack percussion. They bought the few albums they could afford. The rest they handed off to Mary, who stuffed as many as she could up her shirt. (Anyone who patted down a teenage girl, safe to say, would be crucified.)

✳

By the time they staggered back home, it was dark, and when Jay led Darryl back to his house, Darryl didn't even brush his teeth, throwing himself onto his bed and crumbling into the deepest sleep he'd ever experienced.

✳

In the days that followed, Naz was the only thing anyone could think about. Its surreal

Figure 43
They Discovered a Store Overflowing
with "Different" Music.

❋

buffet of humanity was the antidote to their featureless suburban lives. Naz was every lesson you couldn't learn from a book. It's where you went when you were ready.

It all felt to Darryl like a club, a secret club, a club so secret you didn't even know it existed till you were in it.

Jay seemed to feel this way, too. It had even calmed his electric, restless energy. One day at school he pulled up beside Darryl and leaned in close to Darryl's ear and whispered, "Not so much with the night screams anymore."

✺

Jay was the first to change his look to match their newfound cool. He switched his tunic for a pair of filthy pants and a T-shirt. He grew his hair long, like those guys with faraway eyes who wandered Naz's streets babbling, except that in Jay's case, instead of looking insane, it looked . . . insane.

The others immediately followed suit.

Darryl started out with a dandy cummerbund but discarded it when he saw Jay's wide-eyed reaction: "Hey, hey . . . cooool . . ." Darryl let his hair grow over his narrow shoulders. Mary got multiple piercings, a whole range of studs and rings cascading down the sides of her ears.

Jude's hair fell out seemingly overnight, and Jude acted like it was from some sort of dark magic, but Darryl suspected he'd spent too much time dragging his fingers through it aiming for that supercool windblown look, which Darryl completely related to and kind of felt bad for Jude about, but still. Jude got a raven instead. He called it Mike, a name, Jude said, "that came to me in a dream."

Their parents hated their new look. ("I hate your new look," Darryl's mother told him.) When they tomcatted around the neighborhood now, they drew stares of disgust and fear. Families crossed the street whenever they saw them walking around town. Mothers covered their children's eyes. Men did that weird puffed-up-chest, sucked-in-gut thing they do when they're around things that are cooler than they are.

And it was good.

Really good.

✺

One afternoon, Mary pierced Darryl's ear. He was distracted by the fact Mary was within hugging distance, but it still hurt, like, for real, worse than L'il Wade's sting. She told him to leave it alone or else he'd get an infection, but he couldn't help himself from worrying the lobe, which felt so much

Figure 44
"Their Parents Hated Their New Look."

heavier now with a stud stuck through it.

He asked Mary how it looked, and she told him, shrugging, "Swollen," and then, less than a minute later, she said, "Dude, that looks really infected!"

She reached out to touch it, but he flinched away, and even this made his ear feel like it was on fire, like he would be better off if someone just sliced it off completely.

He sent Jay a message: *so much pain . . . so much pus . . . having trouble hearing . . . rooty 2mro?*

Jay wrote back, *ok . . . ?*

All Darryl could do to hide

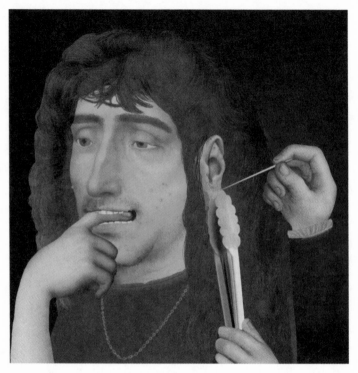

Figure 45
"It Still Hurt, Like, for Real."

his now severely inflamed ear was to pull his hair forward and hope his mother didn't notice or ask him any questions about it.

When Jay got his first good look, he scrunched up his face and said, "That's cool . . . so disgustingly cool," and even just this made it all hurt a little less. "I wanna touch it," Jay said, and Darryl practically screamed, "No, don't!" And Jay laughed and then he said, "Look, check this out."

Jay had shot a bunch of covert footage of some intense protests in Naz. It was hard for Darryl to make out what was going on—the crush of

people, a glancing arm or leg or the side of someone's face, the shouting, the shoving.

"It's real stuff . . . like for *real* real. Writing a song about it," Jay said. He started thumping on his guitar and rapping:

Moneylenders, dented fenders,
way too much sand and diarrhea,
Romans here, Romans there,
people in their underwear!

He went on like this for a while until Darryl, swept up in the moment, added his own verse:

Filthy street, dirty feet,
these poor peeps have naught to eat!

"Nice!" Jay said. "Thinking we call it 'Tree of Life'? But let's keep our song secret secret till it's cooked, okay?"

Darryl agreed. Hearing Jay call his song their song? Well, what to say, except that now Darryl had forgotten all about his silly gangrenous ear.

❧

At band practice, Mary made an announcement:

"So . . . I got us a gig! The school dance! Next week!"

Only Darryl didn't join the group high five. He started to speak, but panic-saliva filled his mouth. In his head, a debate broke out:

— I suck.

— But there'll be girls!

— The band sucks.

— You can wear your new slacks!

— The new slacks make the rash worse!

— Mary sucks for thinking we don't suck.

— If I don't do this, Mary will crack open my skull . . .

Tears started to well up in his eyes, as they did when the going got tough for Darryl and the scenario was moving beyond his meager definition of "no big deal." He looked at Jay, the king of No Big Deal. The king of You Got This. Jay smiled at Darryl and then pointed his finger at Darryl's chest and then his thumb back at his own chest and then mimed a kick-ass explosion with one hand, and then did another one with his other hand.

Figure 46
It Was Hard to Make Out What Was Going On.

Darryl felt his butt un-clench for the first time in years.

After practice, Mary bailed, and Jay announced he had "work to do" and shot Darryl an exaggerated wink on the way out. He did this only because Darryl was not great at picking up hints. Darryl tried to wink back, but he was also not great at winking, and both of his eyes fluttered like he just took a faceful of Mace.

As soon as Jay was gone, Jude mimicked Darryl's eye spasm. "What's up with that?"

"Nothing," Darryl said. Darryl ached to spill the beans.

Figure 47
"Only Darryl Didn't Join the Group High Five."

✳

Jude looked at him. *Seriously?*

"Nothing," Darryl said. He'd promised he wouldn't spill the beans.

"Yeah, as if you've got anything going on," Jude said.

Darryl would definitely never spill the beans. He stared at Jude. Jude stared back.

Then Mike the Raven spread his wings. Like really spread them.

And Darryl spilled the beans.

"We wrote an amazing song about Naz!" Instant regret. But there was no stopping the beans now. "And Jay's probably finishing it as we speak."

Figure 48
The Bird Stared Deep into Darryl's Soul.

Jude's face was a mask. You could see him processing the information. Then he stood up and walked out, leaving Darryl alone with Mike. Darryl stared at Mike. The bird cocked its head and stared back, deep into Darryl's soul. Then it cawed. So very, very terrifying.

Darryl panicked. He needed to fix what he'd done. Somehow tell Jay what had happened, that he was super-sorry. He sent a series of texts:

— *I need to tell you something.*

— *Like really important.*

— *Like really really important.*

His texts went unread though. He wished there was

Figure 49
He Carefully Composed a Text.

✻

another way to get in touch with Jay. But there was not.

Darryl ran all over town, searching for Jay in all their favorite summer haunts — the river, the dump, the Mall of Sumeria, and even Galilanes, the local bowling alley. He ran to Jay's house, and his mother — after asking about Darryl's still very infected ear — said she didn't know where Jay was.

Darryl was stumped, out of ideas. Finally, he sat down and carefully composed a text.

Dear sir, he started. No, no, no. *Hey Bud-o!* Nope, that was worse. He started to type *Wazzzzzzzupppp* but didn't

get past the fourth *z* before deleting that.

To Whom It May Concern . . . Too formal.

Finally, he landed on, *Hey U Wanna Meet?*, and before he could think himself out of it, he tapped "send."

Jay texted right back: *Hey sure @ rooty.*

Of course, Rooty! He had no idea why he'd somehow checked the Mall of Sumeria before going to the most obviously obvious place, but now he wasted no time. He ran all the way there and had so much energy by the time he arrived, he jumped high enough to grab the second branch of the tree.

He climbed to his usual branch but at first didn't see Jay anywhere. He could hear Jay's voice, though, singing, maybe? Coming in faintly and somehow in time with the sounds of his own pounding chest. Sweet.

He looked up higher than either of them had yet dared to climb. And there was Jay. And he *was* singing:

Tree of life, filled with strife . . .

His voice was different, less that raw sound of destruction, more something rasping — still destructive in its own way, just different, like Jay at half potency — but for a second, just the sound of it seemed to make Darryl feel light enough that if he let go of the branch he was holding on to, he would float up to Jay, high above him.

But then another voice cut in, higher-pitched and also higher up in the tree, a voice that lessened the lightness, a voice that made Darryl feel heavy and sweaty.

Olive branches cut . . . like a knife.

Jude.

❧

Of course. Darryl knew. He'd always known. Best friends don't stick around. They died mysteriously with ropes tied around their necks. Or they became new best friends with your own worst enemiend. Wades and Jays didn't stick around. Eventually you lost them, just like you lost

Figure 50
"'Olive Branches Cut . . . Like a Knife.'"
*

everything, except probably your virginity.

Jay spotted Darryl and waved him in. Darryl wasn't sure whether to simply climb up and join them or to throw his voice into the mix, too. Instead he fake coughed and pointed at his throat, and then he pointed at his ear, and then pointed at the ground, and then he started to climb down.

As Darryl reached the bottom, Jay and Jude above him sang in depressingly exquisite harmony, and maybe it was just his imagination, but he could hear them singing the whole walk home.

❊

Darryl skipped the next few days of school to archive his pain in the Kübler-Ross Grief Organizer in his binder.

He blocked off Monday for DENIAL and Tuesday for ANGER. If it were up to him, he would park himself on ANGER for the foreseeable future, but since he had band practice later that week, he'd have to power through. Wednesday he'd bang out BARGAINING by 11 a.m., and hopefully DEPRESSION by 3 p.m., and then cover ACCEPTANCE on his skateboard ride home.

Except all he actually did Monday was endlessly check for messages from Jay that never appeared. So, DENIAL done? Or was he in denial about that, too?

Tuesday was occupied by REGRET and — since nothing in his room sparked joy any longer — a bit of purging.

On Wednesday, he hid under his covers. But all he could see — eyes open, eyes closed — was Jude's smirking face. He spent the rest of the day online bouncing wildly from distractions ("You Won't Believe What Seneca Looks Like Now!") to affirmations ("Yes, You ARE Lovable!") to advice ("Top 10 Ways to Tell Someone You Hate Them").

Then he did some light — okay, heavy — weeping.

Then it was time for band practice.

Figure 51
Darryl Spent the Next Few Days
Archiving His Pain.

As soon as Darryl stepped inside the studio, Jude hugged him, "Hey, bro!" This threw Darryl completely off his game, and he ended up hugging Jude back. It felt kind of nice, actually. His old enemiend.

The studio was dark. A thin beam of light shone down on a lumpy something covered by a sheet. Darryl took a seat beside Mary. Mike the Raven ruffled his wings in some dark corner. Jay was nowhere to be seen.

A drumroll. Jude yanked off the sheet. There was Jay in a tight new T-shirt, and with an equally tight smile on his face.

Figure 52
"WE ARE IRON MESSIAH!"

*

Then another spotlight on Jude, standing at his keyboard, one hand raised in the air, his other hand smashing down on the keys, triggering a robotic "WE ARE IRON MESSIAH!"

Then Jude clapped his hands together. "Jay and I wrote a new song! I call it 'Tree of Life'!" Jude chest-bumped Jay, who bumped back.

Seriously? Chest bumps? Don't even get Darryl started on chest bumps, but just days ago, Jay couldn't blink without Jude making his "too-disgusted-to-be-disgusted" face behind Jay's

Figure 53
Darryl Remembered This Dream.

✳

back, and now they were chest-bumping? Darryl knew in his heart that if he focused his rage on this horrible ritual — and maybe even considered how Jude was probably just looking for a way to get closer to Jay without things getting weird, as he himself had done — he could delay processing Jude's even worse declaration that "Jay and I wrote a new song!," as Darryl was completely unprepared to process that one.

Jude started passing out shirts. He tossed Mary a fitted baby tee, which she threw right back at him, so he gave it to Darryl, who made a mental

Figure 54
Mary Was Doing Her Preshow Warmup.

note to downgrade Jude from "He's All Right" to "Total Wang" in the FRIEND OR FOE? section of his binder before squeezing the shirt over his head.

And maybe if Darryl hadn't been so focused on trying to murder Jude with his eyes, he might have seen Jay's big thumbs-up and goofy grin, and if he hadn't turned so quickly in place in order to stomp out of the studio, he might've noticed Jay trying to tap him on the shoulder, or maybe that wouldn't have mattered at all.

That night, Darryl had a dream. A freaky-deaky dream. Who's to say what it meant,

but unlike most of his dreams, Darryl remembered this one.

❧

The day of the school dance arrived. Everyone was on edge. All morning long, Jude — now wearing a wig to cover his bald head — checked and rechecked the wires to his pyrotechnic display. Darryl fought the urge to curl into a tiny ball and roll away. But as he passed Mary, doing her preshow warmup, he was reminded of a reassuring quote he'd seen on a poster at the school counselor's office:

"Keep Your Friends Close and Your Enemies Closer so You Can Stab Them."

❧

Well. Not everyone was on edge.

Jay was standing outside staring at the last rays of sunlight as the orb dipped below the distant horizon, marveling at the golds and reds and rusts stitched to the sky. Then he spotted an older woman trying to cross a busy intersection, but no one saw her, no one stopped to let her by. Jay jogged across the road, holding his hands up as he did, and the carts came to a halt, and then he extended his hand to the old woman, smiled his Jay smile, and with tentative steps, she crossed with him, and he held her arm as they both made their way to the other side of the road.

She thanked him and then offered him money, which he refused, and then scowled at him and said, "I don't like your shirt, young man. It's *much* too tight." And Jay said, "That's okay, I like it enough for the both of us." She hmphed and was gone, and Jay took one last good look at the disappearing sun and waved goodbye to it before he stepped back inside the school.

But Darryl didn't see any of this, and maybe if he had, things would have gone differently. We'll never know.

And then it was showtime.

❧

The curtain rose. Jude did a deep slide in from the wings,

Figure 55
"Launching Face-Searing Balls of Flame."

⁂

splitting his pants in the process, and then popped up like toast. "Hel-lo, Nebuchadnezzar High!"

Silence.

Then booing.

Apparently, Darryl wasn't the only one who kind of, sort of, totally hated Jude now. Darryl booed a little out of the

side of his mouth, too, even as he felt kind of, sort of, terrible about doing it.

Mary, sensing the dire vibe, counted in the song. Darryl stood frozen in place. He knew they should never have played in front of people, actual real-live people. He wanted to be anywhere, but anywhere, else.

Figure 56
"He Shook His Head Like a Maraca."

*

Then he caught a glimpse of Jay, who was standing in a pool of golden light. He began to sway, and Darryl thought, No, don't sway, people hate swaying, but Jay was swaying so serenely that, despite his best efforts to heed his own advice, Darryl closed his eyes and started to sway, too, just as the band laid down the first chords over the jeers.

He opened his eyes again halfway through the song and realized they had almost convinced the crowd to stop booing, when Jude's fireworks sparked and then shot off. The fireworks were supposed to end the show, punctuate the

final chorus of "Tree of Life," and they certainly weren't supposed to go off, all of them at once, in the middle of their first song, launching face-searing balls of flame that sent the crowd diving for cover.

The fire alarm sounded. Darryl scanned the crowd for the fire marshall. As usual, he knew where the exits were and was preparing to file out of the building in an orderly fashion when . . . he heard Jay's voice. Over the noise of the fireworks, the screams of the people set ablaze in the crowd, Jay was singing. Even louder. Then louder still. And he wasn't about to stop.

With nothing left to lose, the band let loose.

Darryl felt like he was riding a massive sonic wave. At the back of the hall, a sand-bucket brigade materialized. He wanted to tell them, *Don't bother dudes! We'll snuff it out with our sound!* It sounded cool, except the opposite was happening. The fire grew every time Jay wailed away, like he was fanning the flames with his voice.

The whole scene was desperate, intense, oper-atic, a little bit musical. Falling cinders set Darryl's perm ablaze. He shook his head like a maraca, trying to put out the embers, but managed only to ignite them.

The crowd lost its mind.

Forty-three minutes later, the entire school had burned to the ground.

The band sat among the smoking ruins, together, alone, each one of them wishing the fire had consumed them, too, since then they'd be tragic, which seemed to be way better than pathetic.

Or arrested, which was what it seemed like should happen, considering they had burned down a school.

Darryl wiped from his eyes the tahini that had been used as fire suppressant. He poked his thumb through the scorched hole in his new shirt. He had an epiphany:

Maybe I should not have sabotaged Jude's fireworks.

Then Mary said, "Hey."

They all looked up, thinking she was saying "Hey" to someone else, and then looked back at her. She held out her phone. Someone had posted a video of the climax of the night's events.

The video was tagged #IRONMESSUCKIT! Which, to be fair, was a pretty funny hashtag. It had fourteen likes, so Darryl relaxed into the familiar comforts of anonymity.

Mary refreshed her display. This time it had 50,337 likes.

Then 304,560 likes.

A sudden gust of wind lifted the smoke. A man was standing in front of them.

Mary said, "Hey."

"Ronnie," he said, thrusting out his hand. "Band manager." He pointed at Mary's phone. "You guys are gonna be huge."

Figure 57
"'You Guys Are Gonna Be Huge.'"

*

WINTER

Apparently, "huge" meant something different to Ronnie than it did to Darryl. To Ronnie, it seemed to mean "small." They played the Chariot Show 'n' Shine along with a ton of bar mitzvahs, of course, but the real bread and butter for the band was playing the musical accompaniment for crucifixions. These were Jude's favorite. Darryl found them unfulfilling at best, uncomfortable at worst—what if it was someone they knew?—but Ronnie kept them motivated with pep talks filled with profound-seeming advice, like "You have to pay your dues!" He yelled this over and over again to prove how profound it was.

In his binder, under CALCULATIONS, Darryl tried to work out how much the dues were, but he kept arriving at impossibly high numbers, so he moved these pages to a section labeled WHO KNOWS?

Although, who was Darryl to complain? Maybe they weren't famous—"You will be, trust me, kids!"—but they were a lot closer to something like fame—notoriety?—than Darryl had ever imagined for himself. Darryl always assumed if he ever became famous, it would be for being patient zero for a viral plague.

Still, Jude told them all to get ready, their big moment was just around the corner. Darryl spent countless hours in front of the mirror, perfecting his headbanging and performing kegels to improve his pelvic thrusts. Jude forced him to get his nails done, since there'd be "Cameras, dude. Focus on the fretwork, man!" Darryl looked up what fretwork was and worked on this, too.

※

And then, out of the blue, Ronnie got Iron Messiah a three-record deal.

"Sorry it took so long, guys," he told them. "We had to make enough to pay off the families first—the ones whose kids were incinerated during the school dance." Then later

Figure 58
"Jude Told Them All to Get Ready, Their Big Moment
Was Just Around the Corner"

*

that same day, he set up a live gig from a rooftop in Naz.

The label dropped their first album a week later. They'd pressed a scratchy record-ing of the live high school concert, titled it *GYMNASIUM OF DEATH*, and left in all the screaming and roaring sounds of the fire destroying the building — "Street cred," Ronnie explained. Darryl thought it was a bit much, and definitely too soon. But as usual, he was wrong. As soon as the record dropped, Messiah owned this town.

Groupies hid in the trash cans outside Jay's house, and buried themselves in

the sand in his front yard, ready to pop up at the first sign of Jay. One even snuck into Jude's bedroom, a story Jude dined out on for weeks (leaving out that it was Mr. James, the school music teacher, and that he thought it was Jay's bedroom he was sneaking into).

Darryl had no idea he was experiencing a major transformation — or that he'd always wanted to be changed — until suddenly, before he'd even realized the metamorphosis was happening, it was complete. He'd gone from someone whose name often eluded his own father — Darren ... Darden ... Derek! — to a golden duuuude of rock.

He tried to flowchart his feelings:

"Parents Hate Us > Kids Love That Their Parents Hate Us > Kids Love Us > Parents Hate That Their Kids Love Us."

Even to Darryl it didn't seem to track, considering how the parents only needed to stop hating Iron Messiah to bring the whole delicate structure tumbling down. And he wasn't sure what would happen if anyone found out how much Jay's parents loved him, no matter what, or how much he loved them, no matter what.

He put the flowchart away. He knew that if he thought too much about it, it might accidentally all break apart.

❧

Before they knew it, and definitely before they were ready, the rooftop gig was upon them.

They hadn't practiced once since their album was released. For one, anytime they tried to meet for practice, groupies would swarm the practice studio and chant outside or pound on the walls, too loud and insistent to play over.

They could have worn disguises — that had been Darryl's suggestion — but Jude convinced them all they didn't need to practice anyway, and that practice would maybe actually only ruin that raw sound that was so very mesmerizingly raw that no one

Figure 59
He Decided That Being Liked Was Pretty Great.

seemed to care that they had burned down the only school for miles around.

Ronnie hustled them through makeup as an announcement boomed out over the plaza:

"Ladies and serfs. Put your hands together for . . . IRON . . . MESSSIIIIAHHHHHH!"

Darryl felt a sudden rush of shit to the heart. He was right back on his high school stage, his hair in flames. It would be worse, though, this time, his hair shellacked with hair spray—wasn't that stuff flammable?—and the stringy bits missed by the hair stylist stuck to his face, trapped there

by all the makeup, which also smelled faintly of gasoline.

Instinctively, he began shaking his head — and everyone in the crowd started doing the same thing.

No one had ever copied Darryl before. As he looked out at the sea of people, all doing the same thing — his thing — he decided that being liked by people who had no reason to like him was actually pretty great, and he launched into the most earnest solo he'd ever played in his entire life. More earnest than the solo he'd torn into that afternoon he found himself alone in the house and had discovered the soft fuzz of armpit hair. More earnest than the solo he'd ripped the day after he learned about Wade. So earnest, the crowd screamed and wept.

※

They did concerts every few days now, and at each one, the crowds grew exponentially in both numbers and rabidity. They headlined the Road to Damascus Tour and had already been booked for the weeklong end-of-summer RAWK! Festival. As the venues got bigger, the green rooms became ever more luxurious. Jude's fanciful rider requests, like a walk-in safe for his wigs, an engaging treasure hunt for Mike the Raven, and a local posse who would follow him around and laugh at everything he said, were now fulfilled without eye rolls. The insanity became so insane — and this was what was weirdest to Darryl — that it became just normal. Darryl thought, It's like riding a camel, and at first the trot feels both implausible and unsustainable — any minute you're gonna be on the ground, trampled to death by a camel — and then the camel arrives at a gallop, and contrary to what you'd think, things quiet down and you're almost . . . flying?

Not that Darryl had ever been on a camel, of course, due to the recurring and terrifying dream about the one with human teeth, and also

Figure 60
People Loved Jay in That Obsessive Way.

his mother's discomfort at Darryl's proximity to such a pronounced hump—"It's just obscene, Darryl"—but he remembered Jay telling him that this was how it went, that you just had to hold on, and it would all smooth out.

Even though Darryl was convinced people would grow bored of Messiah, they didn't. The more they saw, the more they wanted—especially of Jay.

People loved Jay—no, *really loved* him—in that obsessive way that fell somewhere between souvenir pajamas and restraining order. Darryl was still getting used to having to share Jay with

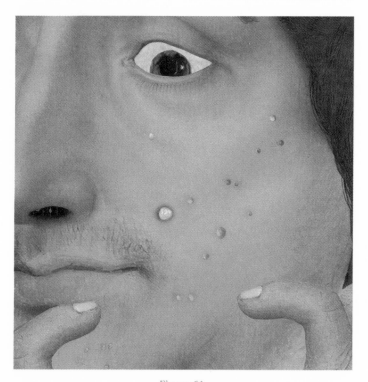

Figure 61
Fame Did Not Fix His Ailments.

Jude. He wasn't quite ready to share him with everyone else.

Jude was jealous of Jay's fame, too, and wanted to be sure he wasn't gonna miss out. He got a tattoo of Jay's face on his back that read, "BFFs Forever!" and went out of his way to be seen with Jay, once even crashing an interview — "Sorry I'm late!" — and squeezing himself into the same chair as Jay.

This made sense to Darryl, even if he didn't approve of Jude's methods, and even when he remembered that he and Jude used to be much closer.

In his quest to be wholly

unremarkable, he'd ensured the clothes his mother made him were the exact color of the local sand. He did his best to follow a few beats behind the newest trends. He couldn't afford actual headphones like the ones all the kids were wearing, but he fashioned a mock pair out of one of his mom's old brassieres and woven palm fronds, and he wore them whenever he was out on his own. Whenever anyone told him what their favorite thing was — band, color, food, type of pencil — he'd be sure to nod right away and say, "Yeah, that's my favorite, too."

Even with Jay, Darryl tried his best to be unnoticed. Darryl remembered a time when they went to the beach, and the sand was too hot for Darryl's tender tootsies. Jay piggybacked him the whole way to their picnic spot. When they'd reached the far end, Darryl looked back at the single line of footprints in the sand, smiled, and thought, Huh. It's like I was never even here. Cool, I guess?

There were a few moments when he had taken a stand and performed small, almost imperceptible acts of defiance. Like when he pinched wrapped muffins or chocolate bars in the store, the ones that had a gooey center — those were the best. It wasn't an FU to the store, or to the insidiousness of big sugar, but to chase a feeling he found hard to stop chasing, a feeling of making a little mark somehow.

Boop.

So it was somewhat of a surprise — and not necessarily the best kind — when he realized he was maybe worse than invisible and insignificant: he was famous.

There were hordes of fans who wept and wailed whenever Messiah was spotted in public. Darryl felt super-loved whenever someone fainted in front of him the first few times it happened. But then he noticed that if he looked in their eyes before they fell in a convulsing heap, their face grimaced, just a little, but also

they didn't seem to be looking at him, not really. They were mostly looking through him. Maybe at Jay? It wouldn't have mattered anyway.

For one, being famous didn't fix his ailments. All the hysteria and rashes and worry hives and vapors persisted and in some cases even got worse. Sure, now there was a team of specialists to help manage them — the skin division replaced his off-brand salves with high-end creams filled with camel placenta, whipped mousse of myrrh, and other fancy stuff — but these only made his sores seep something fierce. And the consultants could say all they wanted about his chi rebalancing itself — seeping sores weren't cool. (They filled his pockets with crystals to help expedite the alignment, so now he made a tinkling sound whenever he took a step. They also prescribed a lubricant to prevent the crystals from chafing his thighs.)

The thing Darryl had always assumed would come with becoming famous — a girlfriend — seemed even more out of reach than before. The only female he'd ever really kissed besides his mom was Dead Donna, the CPR dummy they practiced doing mouth-to-mouth on in gym class, and even with her, he could not get her heart beating again, no matter how hard he tried.

Some days he caught himself thinking back to the girl with blue hair from the Flutes and Lutes Festival. She seemed like someone who could laugh at herself, all footloose and fancy-free, which was a trait — maybe the only trait? — he looked for in the girls he thought he might someday attempt to date. If they could laugh at themselves, it seemed much less likely they would laugh at him.

Other days, he remembered that the real reason he had so very badly wanted a girlfriend was simply because he so very badly wanted a friend.

Figure 62
"Darryl Normally Loved Fine Print."

Jude spent a lot of time with MGMT—industry-speak (he informed Darryl) for "management." Before long, Jude and Ronnie were besties, whispering things in each other's ear, texting each other constantly.

The more Jude and Ronnie talked, the more important-looking documents seemed to materialize for the band to sign. No one really read them: Jay trusted everyone, and Mary refused to sign anything for anyone.

Darryl normally loved fine print—his favorite part of getting powerful new medication was poring over the

Figure 63
"Darryl Thought Back to Simpler Times."

†

endless list of microscopic contraindications like it was a horoscope—but in this case, he couldn't be bothered. He would have thrown away all their fame for a lazy hour in Rooty with Jay, just the two of them. But Ronnie said all lazy hours had to be requisitioned through him.

Jude kept them all apart, to "keep things fresh," which Darryl thought was maybe unnecessary, and some practicing together would be smart? "But practicing together," Jude said, "will just ruin the spontaneity of that first time Jay started wailing in the middle of our song, man, right?"

Most of all, Darryl was missing Jay real bad and would send him texts every ten minutes — *miss u*; *Freaky times, right?* — but they all came back with the same response, *Hey Superfan! Thanks so much for reaching out! I'm real busy, but I'll be sure to look over your request and respond in the order it was received!*, which didn't sound like Jay, but Darryl kept trying anyway.

Darryl thought back to simpler times and how they were so very different from the "Big Times." Even worse, his life was scheduled to the minute now, and he could no longer sleep in or even go on one of his dérives. He asked if he could meet Jay at Rooty maybe? But Jude had deemed Rooty a security risk. Whenever Darryl tried to do anything, the bodyguard Jude had assigned him would shake his head. *No way, little man.*

Having protection was new, too. It meant bullies were no longer an issue. But bullies were supposed to be key to how Darryl understood where he was situated on his Alpha to Omega Male Scale. So what now?

Also — and this might have just been him — was it weird that the bodyguard was always facing him?

🦋

Then Ronnie called a band meeting.

"Jude's got some terrific ideas to share," he said.

The lights dimmed. Some motivational music swelled as Jude strode in wearing a headset and waving a laser pointer. "Let me take you on a journey," he said, starting the slideshow. Darryl sighed his heaviest sigh, but nobody noticed over the music.

As Jude's vision of the band's future unfolded — slide after slide after slide — on the screen behind him, Darryl imagined a different version of their past: Jude going up in smoke at the school fire, in place of that nice redheaded Mesopotamian kid, and everyone drinking posca down by

the canal instead of sitting here listening to this inane presentation.

Jude continued to roll out his ridiculous fantasy, and as he did, Darryl noticed it became more focused, exclusive, like he was delivering it to an audience of one—and it wasn't to Darryl or Mary or Ronnie or even Mike the Raven.

The slides started out featuring illustrations of the entire band, but as Jude showed how things would be "improved," Darryl and Mary became more crudely drawn, and less prominent, until they had faded out completely, leaving only ornately detailed versions of Jay and Jude in the picture.

And by the end, Jude was sitting right in front of Jay, leaning in, kneeling actually, whispering directly and only to him.

"Now, Jay, you'll agree that the music is important, right? And you can't deny that the message is what it's all about? Jay—what we're delivering is a truth the people need to hear. Right, Jay?"

Darryl tried staring extra-hard at Jay, hoping he'd snap him out of the trance he appeared to be in. Troublingly, Jay appeared to be digging it and interjected, "The music has to stay true to the people who inspired it."

"Yeah, yeah, the amazing people of Naz!" Jude said, standing. His work here was done. "Ronnie has asked me to direct a new video. We'll tell *their* story—the actual people of Naz will be the stars."

Mary nodded in appreciation. It might have been that Jude's pitch had worked on her, too, or she might just have been high on the mushrooms she often took to keep Jude at a distance.

The next morning, Darryl's mom said, "Isn't that your little friend from next door on the television?"

And there was Jay, his little friend from next door, being interviewed before a live

Figure 64
"Jude's Vision of the Band's Future Unfolded."

audience on *The Morning Show for Naz with Dazz!* It was surreal, as Darryl had never seen someone he knew on television. He thought it was like the magic box had somehow stolen his friend's soul and miniaturized it for everyone — even people who'd never met him — to enjoy. He knew this was a stupid thing to think, but he thought it anyway.

Jay was, as they say, on message, or, rather, on Jude's message.

"The music has got to stay true to the people who inspired it — the people of Naz," he said.

The host followed up: "Yes, the music. We've never heard

Figure 65
And There Was Jay, Darryl's Little Friend, on TV.

✻

anything like it before. Can you tell us about your process?"

Jay paused for a second, and Darryl could see his mind whirling, then kick into overdrive. "Well, you know in metal shop at school, when you're smelting iron? And the furnace is so hot—you can't stand there for more than a few seconds without your arm hairs burning up, and you feel like your face is going to melt off and Mr. James is yelling that you have to put the ingots in, now, or else you can't make the ashtray and you'll fail, right? It's like that. We're making metal. We have to. Or else we'll burst into flames." It seemed he had said all he needed to say, and then he added, "And if we don't, we've failed."

"Amazing," she answered dreamily. "What—or who, maybe?—have you failed, exactly?"

"Well," Jay started to say, and then he looked up, and then he looked straight at the camera, but to Darryl it seemed as if Jay were looking straight at him, that finally—only through the miracle of television—Darryl and Jay could look at each other the

way they'd looked at each other through the dense upper branches of Rooty. "We failed . . ." and for that second Jay seemed lost, and looked extremely tired.

Jay was at a loss for words. Jay was never at a loss for anything. Jude, who'd been sitting out of the frame beside him, leaned in.

"We failed to remind you to . . . buy tickets to our Rock the Cradle of Civilization Tour!"

The audience screamed.

"The tour will take us back to our roots—in fact the first stop will be at the actual tree where Jay and I wrote 'Tree of Life.' And there'll be an epic surprise! And what Jay said about the metal, I was totally going to say that if you'd asked me. Metal!"

Epic surprise? Rock the dreidel of what? When did this become the plan? And why was Darryl hearing about it on TV with the help of his little friend from next door, of all people? He had to admit the word "metal" as a

descriptor of their music sounded pretty cool though.

※

They began prepping for the video shoot that afternoon. A stage floated in a fog-machine cloud. Dozens of salt-mine slaves Jude had brought in to perform the dance routines started limbering up, the thin layer of salt dust making their every movement squeak.

Jude strode in, bullhorn in hand. Darryl went to ask him the one million questions he had about the TV appearance, and the surprise, and the dreidel thing, but Jude waved him away and then screamed into the bullhorn, "Let's get this party started, bitches!"

Darryl rolled his eyes so hard he was sure he'd somehow sprained them.

Fake lightning bounced around the rafters.

"Mary—snarly face!" Jude barked. "Jay—perfect. Just perfect!" "Give it up, Darryl! Bam bam in the ham! Use your knees! Remember your kegels! More anger!" Darryl—

humiliatingly humping the air while saying *Freekeh!* in his head, singing stolen lyrics, taking orders from the guy who had filched his BFF—did not feel he needed help with anger. *I'll show you anger.*

He raised his bass and smashed it down again and again, until all he was holding was a splintered stump.

In the awkward silence that followed, Ronnie leaned across and whispered in Jude's ear.

"Darryl, thank you for your input," Jude said to Darryl, and waited while Ronnie whispered more into his ear. "Your feedback has been noted."

※

Later, rage was coursing through Darryl's body. It was an odd sensation, warm and prickly, like after he was given new meds for his lumps and bumps, and the unfamiliar chemicals were percolating through his body, at once making him happy to think that they were working but also kind of scared they might go too far. And kill him.

He wrote Jay, who for sure could make sense of this sensation. There was no better balm than Jay's soothing words. Jay replied right away, *Busy*. Not soothing or balm-like at all.

It made no sense to Darryl that Jay was acting the way he was acting, that he was too busy for Darryl. He wanted to write Jay, *What the hell, man?* But he'd never sworn at Jay, ever—he just didn't seem like the kind of guy you swore around, especially not in the minefield of misinterpretation of text messages, and definitely not to a friend he was already afraid of losing. Instead, he started a new section in his binder, WHAT THE H-E-DOUBLE-HOCKEY-STICKS, JAY?, and started filling it with any clue that might explain Jay's change from an awesome guy into, well, a dickface.

He thought long and hard, waggling his pen between his fingers.

There was that time he overheard Jay and Jude working on a song, and Jay off the

Figure 66
"'Let's Get This Party Started, Bitches!'"

top of his head came up with a sweet verse:

It gets a little easier each time you make things change.

But each time you change things, you change all things.

Jude was nodding his head in appreciation. "Awesome . . . but what if we change the lines to *One two. One two three. Won't.*

You. Look. At. Me! Jay looked at him in the same semi-tired, half-smiling way he'd looked that one time at a blind dog that kept walking into walls. He sang Jude's new lyrics, of course, and made even the idiotic words sound good.

Writing this down was helpful, Darryl thought.

Figure 67
Epic.
‡

So he decided to send it all to Jay in a text.

He spent the rest of the day checking his messages, waiting for Jay to receive it. Darryl's least favorite aspect of messaging — and this probably applied to other areas of his life as well — was the anticipation, since he filled such moments with worst-case scenarios. His therapist called this his "anxietycipation," but Darryl was sure this wasn't a real thing, even if it felt like it should be.

After what seemed like forever, the status changed to Delivered, and then to Read, and then the best part, the little ellipses drumroll. It hung there for a good long while. This was gonna be epic, Darryl thought. But then it hung there long enough for Darryl's anxiety to slip back into gear, triggering the not-great memory of the ellipses on the day that Wade died, filled with promise, then with pain. As if on cue, the dots went away in Jay's text, too. And no response followed, even though Darryl waited. And that was definitely not in any way epic.

Darryl thought of all the ways he could figure out what was up with Jay. He tried sending him good vibes, but that just made Darryl sweaty, and now his bed was all soppy. He sat up and walked over to the window, and through it he saw Jay's mom.

She was out in the garden, tending to an impossibly fertile-looking tomato plant. He realized he had never actually eaten a tomato, as his mother never put them on the grocery list. Now that he saw their very ripe redness, tender skin, and juicy flesh, he understood why she thought they might be, well, problematic. *And besides, I think you're allergic to nightshades*, he imagined her saying. Used to be, Jay was out there helping her with the dirt and the raking and shoveling. But Jay had been so busy with the

band lately, Darryl couldn't remember the last time he'd seen him at his house helping his parents out.

He didn't have anything better to do, so Darryl thought maybe he could help instead. You know, lend a hand.

As soon as he approached, Jay's mother said, "Hello, Darryl. We've missed you," without even turning around. When she did turn toward him, her glowy face was off the hook. She was holding a freshly picked tomato, which she extended to Darryl. This made his own face very red and problematic indeed, and he took the fruit, so warm and tender — there was no way this thing was a vegetable, he thought — and tucked it into the secret inner pocket in his tunic where he kept his lunch money and his best inhaler, which he pulled out and took a big drag from.

After that bit of business was over, Jay's mom said, "I know why you're here. He's been very different lately,

hasn't he? The other night at dinner, we asked him to clear the plates, and he said, 'Is it my turn?' even though he knows that Tuesdays and Thursdays are always his turn. And there are other things. He's been looking at himself all the time, in the mirrors, of course, but also the cutlery, any shiny objects he can find, really, and the other day, I went into his bedroom. I thought he was out. I caught him . . . you know . . . doing a selfie, I think it's called? His father and I are worried. You must be sick with worry. You look sick with worry. Do you have a fever?" She reached out. And. Touched. His. Forehead.

Darryl didn't remember much after that.

※

Later that day, Darryl went round to Ronnie's office. He wanted to apologize for his actions during the video shoot. He'd wrecked a lot of things in his life, but never so intentionally or effectively. But also? Also, he wanted to make a few

things clear about what he thought about the new direction the band was going in, about Jude's role, about the song he (not Jude!) wrote with Jay while high up in Rooty, and maybe, if there was time, and if Ronnie recognized the seriousness of the situation, offered to make a pot of acacia tea, and offered a plate of cookies—this was how Darryl had always imagined he would act as a "kick-ass producer" when one of his stars came to him with a serious problem—maybe then he'd tell Ronnie about Rooty and how it was, most important, his and Jay's tree, and had nothing at all to do with Jude, or even the band.

But when he knocked on Ronnie's door, no one answered. He knocked again, a little louder, and this time the door creaked open. Ronnie wasn't there. He knew he should leave, and in fact turned to leave, but Darryl wanted to know what it was like inside a record producer's office.

It was not what he was expecting. For one, there seemed to be nothing with which to brew a calming pot of tea. It smelled less like freshly baked cookies and more like long-ago-burnt cookies.

But then, before he could make any sense of that, his attention was pulled to the wall above the desk. But not just above the desk. All over the office. Plans and drawings covered every wall. Pictures were pinned to a corkboard— headshots of Mary and Jude and Jay and himself, but also pictures of himself he didn't recognize, and when he looked more closely at them, all set to be enraged and flattered by Ronnie's voyeurism, he realized they *were not* pictures of him, but were of dudes who looked so much like him, they could've been him.

But worst of all, on a whiteboard, on top of a cheap-looking clip art star that was on the pastel spectrum of orange were the words: LIP. SYNC. THE. TOUR!!

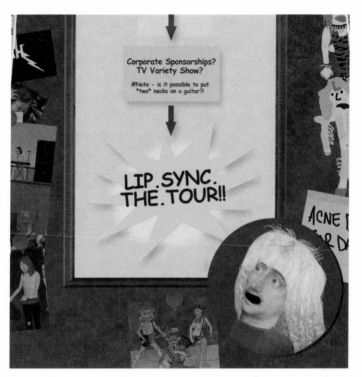

Figure 68
The Camera Was Trained on His OMG Face.

What Darryl did not see was the security camera, trained on his OMG face.

Darryl wrote a quick note — "I'd really like to talk!" — and slipped it under the door as he left, and then he went to find Jay, but for the rest of the afternoon, Jay's assistants kept telling Darryl he was busy, and Darryl could see he *was* busy fulfilling Jude's unending to-do list — photo shoots, costume fittings, signing piles of merchandise — in the conveniently out-of-earshot distance, and by the time he found Jay by himself, not busy or out of earshot, he was sitting on the greenroom couch.

Darryl called out, "Jay!" but as he approached, he realized Jay was sleeping. He looked kind of gray, hollowed out. Darryl didn't have the heart to disturb him, especially with such horrible news.

He wrote Jay a sticky note — "I'd really like to talk . . . ?" — and patted it gently on his shirt so as not to wake him.

※

Later that night, his phone rang. The caller ID said "Jay," so he answered right away, "Hey, Jay!" even though they'd never called each other on the phone. How old were they? Thirty? But the voice on the line didn't sound like Jay. It was quiet and mangled, full of a scratchiness, and not the cool, world-weary scratch Jay did so effortlessly but a difficult and painful scratch, and Darryl couldn't even understand what Jay was saying. Then there was the sound of fumbling and stumbling in the background, and when someone spoke again, this time it wasn't Jay; it was Jay's junior assistant. "Darryl, Stan here. Jay wanted to call in response to your latest communication, but his voice is wrecked, man, just wrecked." Darryl heard Jay's hoarse voice in the background, and for whatever reason, Darryl could understand him better than when he had been on the phone: "Tell him I'm worried about him and ask him what was up with that crazy smashing-bass thing. Oh, and that I have a sore throat from all the interviews." Jay's junior assistant whispered into the phone, "Darryl, Jay thinks you've gone a bit crazy, and Jude has recommended that maybe it's best you two stay apart for a while." Darryl said, "Oh." Stan covered the phone and yelled to Jay, "Darryl says no problem!" Darryl wanted to say that that was not what Jay had said, and not what he had said either, but he gave Stan the benefit of the doubt, since, hey, he was Jay's junior assistant, and you don't get to be that without some serious chops.

Darryl remembered a moment from the summer when there was no intermediary between them, no chance of miscommunication or misinterpretation. It was just him and Jay shooting hoops. They were there for hours, and Jay never missed once, and Darryl never missed once either, and Darryl wished it was still that day.

Stan whispered to Darryl, "Thanks for calling, Darryl, great talk, we'll be in touch real soon," and hung up before Darryl could say that Jay had in fact called him, that it wasn't at all a great talk, and that these two facts didn't bode well for the promise he'd be in touch with Jay anytime real soon.

✻

The next person who got in touch was Ronnie, calling him into his office. MGMT was obviously taking his note seriously, he thought, pleased.

He'd spent all night figuring out what he was going to say, how terrible it would be to rob their fans of Jay's soul-crushing voice — the recordings sounded cool, of course, nothing could make Jay sound uncool, but his recorded voice didn't ripple through the air, didn't make you feel like your body was being torn into pieces and reintegrated into the subatomic particles from which you were born (in a good way!), not the way Jay's voice live did. It was like the difference between being in the middle of an awesome sandstorm and watching a webcam feed of one. Darryl had done both, and believe you me, he knew which was more memorable.

He cleared his throat. He knocked. He cleared his throat again. And when the door opened, he found himself staring at Jude.

Jude smiled and stepped aside to let Darryl in. He didn't see Ronnie anywhere. Before he could say anything, Jude held up a copy of the contract.

"Okay, Darryl, breaks my heart to say this," Jude said. "A

Figure 69
"Jay Never Missed Once, and Darryl Never Missed Once Either."

✝

few things . . . it clearly states, in chapter 419, verse 2, of the contract, 'Thou shalt not destroy band equipment and/or introduce bad vibes,' blah blah blah blah, amen, you can read the exact language on your own. Anyway."

Ronnie's hand shot out of a little blanket fort that Darryl hadn't even noticed until now, holding a thick folder. Darryl screamed in surprise, then after he composed himself, thought, So *that's* a power move. Wow.

"Thanks, Ronnie, man," Jude said, and took the package. "This is your file. Really, there've been a lot of

Figure 70
"When the Door Opened, He Found
Himself Staring at Jude."

infractions, and we've over-
looked them, you know,
because Jay likes you, thinks
you're his friend. But the thing
yesterday with the bass — "

"And breaking into my
office," Ronnie's muffled voice
said from the cozy confines of
the blanket fort.

"And for breaking into
Ronnie's office, thanks, don't
want to forget that — anyway,
it's the straw, you know, the
one last straw that breaks the
straw-slave's back."

Jude held the file out for
Darryl to take but Darryl
wouldn't take it. If he touched

it, he thought, that would make it all real, or at least make it look like he was okay with this. But he wasn't okay with this.

"The band took a vote, man," Jude said gently. Darryl could see an unfamiliar flicker in his eyes. It wasn't quite sympathy, not quite pity, but more a *Things could have gone a different way between us, right?* kind of look. Jude continued, "Jay wasn't there, since we don't bother him with petty things, but we're pretty sure we know how he would have voted. Mary abstained, so Mike was the tiebreaker. Majority rules. You're out."

Ronnie's hand emerged again from the fort, this time with a gift basket, including a Jay-themed BBQ apron silk-screened with the words "Who Wants a Hot One?" with a matching ball cap.

❧

Darryl felt sick, and hurt, and angry, and lost. Even though he was used to feeling at least one of these emotions,

he wasn't used to handling them all at once. A deep, dark sadness was rising up in him. It felt scary and familiar, like that one time with Wade.

Darryl and Wade had had a running reference in which they'd say, "And he's, like," and pretend they'd hung themselves, standing, slowly twisting, heads down, black and lifeless stares, arms useless by their sides. The first time he and Wade played at this, Darryl could feel his stomach and insides knotting as he tried to "No, no, no, make it look real, like, really real," as Wade suggested, sticking his own purple tongue — how'd he get it to be so purple? — out of his bloated-looking face. And sure, after a while, Darryl learned to laugh at Wade telling him how it'd be funny if they put a note on the door that said, DO. NOT. OPEN. THE. DOOR. and rigged it so that if the door were opened, it would pull a chair out from under them and hang them. And sure, eventually Darryl figured out it was

a dark kind of humor that you could perform only with a close, trusted friend like Wade. But right after that first time, Wade had asked him, "Was that weird, was it too weird?" and Darryl had said, "Kind of?" and Wade's face had turned dark and toothless, and Darryl said, quickly, "No, just kidding, that was awesome," and Wade smiled and said, "Cool, 'cause we're going to do it again, maybe with actual rope this time. Ha ha."

In that moment between the moments, when Wade's face had turned dark and toothless and when Darryl had lied about how he felt, the feeling he had felt in that brief blip was the feeling he was feeling right now.

⁂

Darryl needed to talk to Jay. Jay had to know. Darryl wondered, Did he know? Had his junior assistant briefed him? He ran to Jay's house. There was a huge line of people—including the stars of the Rich Kids of Rome, who were #SlummingIt—all

waiting their turn at his window. Hired muscle managed the queue. Darryl pulled his new hat down tight so no one would recognize him as an integral member of the band, and his disguise worked incredibly well.

By the time Darryl reached the front, the sun had set and it was dark and getting darker. Jay looked wrecked, even more wrecked than the last time he'd seen him asleep looking so wrecked. And for a half second, Darryl thought, He should rest, I should let him rest, but no. Not this time. This is too important.

Jay said, "Darryl." And then he paused, for a long enough time that Darryl didn't know where he was going with this.

And so, Darryl uncorked.

"Jude is destroying what your music is all about and you kicked me out of the band for smashing the bass? Which wasn't even a real bass! And for wrecking the vibe? Which wasn't even real, either!"

Jay locked in on Darryl.

Figure 71
"Darryl Uncorked."

Shock flashed through his eyes. Which only made Darryl angrier still—an anger fueled maybe by his own guilt at throwing his anger at his only friend—but didn't Darryl have the right to be angry? The right to stand up for himself and what he thought was best for him, for Jay, for the band?

"We're giving people something to believe in—"

"You're not!" Darryl snapped. "You're using Messiah to hawk sunscreen and bath mats. You're a sell-out!" He hesitated, but only for a second. "And a—" And here he mouthed a word he'd never even said out loud

Figure 72
Darryl's Network Was Small, His Talent for Malice Amateurish.

*

before. Jay could of course read lips, and he fully understood.

The fury in Jay's eyes shaded into something else: disappointment.

"You know," Jay said, his voice sounding hollow and far away. "You know how I always say love thy neighbor? I'm taking that one back."

Darryl's eyes went wide, his throat went dry, and his tongue seemed to expand in his mouth so that he couldn't even speak, not that he had any idea what he would say.

But just as quickly, Jay's eyes softened and his face fell. "Oh, Darryl," he said. Except Darryl could have sworn he

said it in the voice they'd reserved for Mickey.

"Time's up," Jay's junior assistant said, sliding the curtain closed between them with the authority of a real junior assistant.

❧

Darryl spent the next morning creating clever, angry memes. He was sure they'd go viral, humiliate Jay, ruin the band, and ease his own pain. But Darryl's social network was so small and his talent for malice so lame, they just fizzled.

He spent some time with his binder, reflecting on how it was always there for him, the sponge for his rage, misgivings, self-doubt, and also the tears that were currently streaming down his face.

Darryl wandered, numb and oblivious to the world around him. He found himself in downtown Naz. It was almost unrecognizable. New shops lined the streets — Muffin Messiah, Messiah Mufflerz, even a Happy Ending Messiah Massage where the Sound Sack store had been.

On the streets, everyone was wearing ridiculous wigs and makeup, even babies and old men. Worst of all was the pan-flute arrangement of "Killer! Summer!" being piped into speakers strung above the street. Messiah Muzak.

He thought about his flowchart, but he'd been wrong about that, too. The "parents" didn't "hate us" anymore, but maybe that was because all the variables had changed? Anyway, that didn't matter. Messiah was all anyone seemed to care about now.

Darryl felt gutted. He needed to do something. But now that he was out of the band, what could he do?

❧

A strong wind whipped down the street, and the answer hit him right between the eyes.

"Are You Poor? Tired? Do You Enjoy Huddled Masses?" read the flyer that had just blown into his face. "If so, Iron Messiah needs YOU as an extra at our next concert!

If you can't be somebody, be some body. (Lepers welcome.)"

Darryl arrived well before the appointed time but still found himself swimming in a crush of people hoping to get cast as extras. He had done his best to look like other hopeful street people lined up in Rooty's shadow. He also had an idea what Jude and Ronnie would be looking for — the right "look" of torn and muddied tunic, mismatched and patched-together sandals — and as the pièce de résistance, he pulled on the "Who Wants a Hot One?" apron to match his hat, knowing they would like that he had his own swag, which would even save them a little money.

With a brisk nod from Ronnie, who had never really recognized him anyway, Darryl was hired as an extra.

And just like that, he was kind of, sort of back in the band.

※

For the next few days, Darryl paraded alongside his fellow Nazarenes as they tried to learn Jude's elaborate "Beggars Can't Be Choosers" choreography, which Jude was directing with a whip that he'd spent some time introducing as "the same one my dad used on the slaves when they were building my studio." A flunky was dousing extras in street slop to make them look even more desperate, but when it came around to Darryl's turn, the flunky shook his head and said, "Nah, he's good." And he *was* good.

Jay and Mary appeared occasionally onstage. They mimed along to the auto-tuned songs while banging away on instruments that weren't even plugged in. He saw a dude saunter onstage, a dude who was just like him, except with the ability to saunter. Darryl remembered the pictures of the Darryl doppelgängers he'd seen tacked to the wall in Ronnie's office. This guy was the worst of the lot, wearing shiny makeup with exaggerated drawn-in acne and a frizzy-perm wig, and drinking

Figure 73
Darryl Had an Idea About the Right "Look."

✻

from Real Darryl's mug. Real Darryl felt honored, jealous, and grossed out all at once.

In his mind, he heard Jay: *We're giving people something to believe in.*

Seriously, Jay?

❧

Darryl excelled at being invisible. It had been his special talent his entire life—and he should've known things would go south with Jay simply based on how Jay always tried to take away his special talent. But now he was comfortably back in his unnoticeable, unremarkable wheelhouse, which was how he overheard Jude explaining his big idea to Mary.

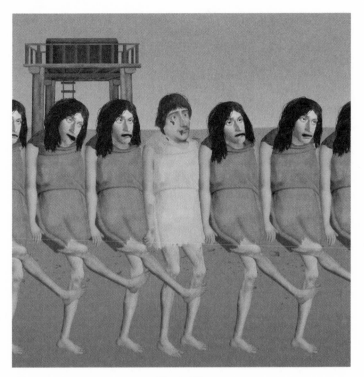

Figure 74
"Darryl Paraded Alongside His Fellow Nazarenes."

*

"You really wanna know what the surprise is, doncha?"

She didn't.

"I'm going to set fire to the dumb tree, man!"

"You mean Rooty?" Mary asked, concerned for maybe — no, definitely — the first time by something that Jude had said.

"Whatever. Who names a tree, man?" Jude whispered. "And who cares? It's about the symbolism. Ashes and rebirth! Trees and seeds! All that crap! Plus, it'll look amazeballs!"

Darryl was so shocked by this, he felt himself become almost fully noticeable. He calmed himself and receded

into the crowd and looked around for Jay, who stood at the edge of the stage, gently tracing his finger along the palm of one of the roadies, who looked like he would melt into the stage from contentment.

Does Jay know? he wondered.

He must. It was his band, too. And his tree.

That night, after rehearsal, Darryl hid under the stage and worked himself into a tizzy. He was furious at Jay for abandoning him, contemptuous of Jude for ruining the purity of the music, confounded that the people of Naz would be so naive to fall for it, and heartbroken that Jay would let Rooty be destroyed. And also let their friendship be destroyed. And in this whirl of emotions, he hatched a plan. He tried to cackle, evil-genius style, but ended up in a phlegmy coughing fit that lasted for several minutes. He'd never been good with laughter of any kind.

He reached under his tunic and felt around for the binder he'd carefully duct-taped there. He tore it off without so much as a flinch and set to work.

❧

It took him the full three days leading up to the concert to finalize his plans. He spent those days living on the pizza crusts and bongwater that filtered through the stage-planks into his hidey hole. Darryl felt animalistic, all nerves, his senses heightened to an almost unbearable degree. He felt like he did when he was going into the cafeteria with his mom's World-Famous Egg Salad warming in a pita in his hoodie pocket — but not in that "they can all smell my World-Famous Egg Salad and they know it's mine and now I'm gonna barf and this is a horrible place to barf" kind of way. Now, instead of vicious gossip from the dudes in the far corner, he could hear locusts swarming a hundred miles away. He could sense the movements of the sand dunes outside Naz. Rooty's long, thirsty roots, he could

Figure 75
"'You Really Wanna Know What the Surprise Is, Doncha?'"

feel them, too, digging deeper and deeper into the earth.

His binder bulged with checklists, blueprints, and flowcharts that were heartbreakingly beautiful in their simple, confident elegance.

On the night of the concert, he watched as thousands of fans filtered in, dressed in identical shirts they'd purchased from the pop-up stands that ringed the stadium.

He resisted the urge to climb onto the stage and tell them all to go home, to forget everything they knew about Iron Messiah, that they were all fools, sheep being led to a postcapitalist slaughter, but

Figure 76
"Darryl Felt Animalistic."

he knew it would do no good. People want to sheep.

The world had moved beyond the power of mere words. The world would be influenced only by action.

The stage grew dark. A dry-ice thundercloud formed in the rafters and hung among Rooty's uppermost branches. Strobe lights pulsed all around, causing the crowd to ooh and aah. And out of the darkness, Jude's voice growled through the loudspeakers:

In the beginning . . . there was nothing . . .

And then . . . there was . . . something . . .

Figure 77
"'ROCKTHECRADLEOFCIVILIZASHHUUUUUUN!'"

A guitar chord ripped open the silence.

"ROCKTHECRADLEOFCIVI-LIZASHHUUUUUUN!"

The prerecorded spectacle exploded with a new song called "1, 2, 3, Look at Me!"

Jude pranced across the stage, windmilling on his keytar. Mary beat the air with her drumsticks, while Jay lip-synched screams. The crowd bought it, raising horn hands to the sky.

"I LOVE YOU, DARRYL!" a young woman screamed at Fake Darryl—which Real Darryl noted had never happened to him—and Fake Darryl mouthed back, *I love you!*

He looked ancient, like he was at least fifty years old.

This action thing was hard. Darryl had so many thoughts about what he was seeing right now, he could have spent a week dissecting them in his binder, and even then this much conflict and inner turmoil would have kept him and Jay in the tree all day, sorting the rest of it out. They would have had to pack a lunch *and* probably dipped into the snacks they kept hidden in a hollow in the tree. But there were no good flat surfaces for him to properly lay out his binder, and his time in the tree with Jay had obviously passed. He did what he did best: he bottled it up and buried it deep inside him, right beside the place where he imagined his eventual ulcer would take root.

Darryl waited. The fog thickened, as he knew it would. He had done several simulations, and proved the exact pattern and timing of fog thickening. Fake Darryl vanished into the fog, as he had hypothesized. He'd studied the choreography for the past three days, knew the two-second beat during which Fake Darryl would be standing directly on top of an unseen trapdoor he'd unlocked before the band took the stage.

Moments later, Real Darryl ascended in Fake Darryl's place, continuing to "play" without dropping a note. Nobody noticed the switcheroo. Operation Expose Messiah was proceeding as planned.

Jude and Jay performed their moronic shtick — back-to-back, closing their eyes on cue, selling the "rapture" thing. Up close, Darryl realized that what he thought were thick smudges of deep-red makeup under Jay's eyes were in fact ridiculous lipstick prints. The whole thing was enough to make Darryl sick with righteous indignation.

What made him angriest was that none of them seemed to recognize that what had

made them famous to begin with was the straight-up raw sound they'd invented, and that by sifting out its best bits and covering up their person- alities with silly costumes they were the opposite of what they'd promised to their fans, and to one another, really.

Darryl scooted across the stage behind them, pulling the cords out of the instruments along the way. Then he also seized the mic stand they were supposedly singing into and started waving the cords all around, knowing for sure that the audience would notice the instruments weren't plugged in, that nothing happen- ing onstage was in any way connected to the music they were hearing.

They didn't notice a thing.

But Jude did.

❧

They locked eyes. Jude's were sizzling with fury, worried that the crowd would come to their senses at any moment. Darryl's were filled with tears, since he hadn't modeled this scenario,

had not imagined actually looking in his old enemiend's eyes like this.

Jude smiled, revealing a few new gold teeth, reached down, and pressed a button on his codpiece.

Somehow, Darryl had missed the codpiece. Likely because of his aversion to looking down, an instinctual by-product of his mother's always telling him, "My eyes are up here, Darryl." He had no idea what the button would do until he saw the top of Rooty light up, revealing a cartoonish bomb and a digital sundial that began counting down.

60, 59, 58 . . .

The music cut out.

Which was when Jay opened his eyes. He saw Darryl, who was still staring up at the bomb and the sundial, and Jay looked up, too.

"Rooty?" Jay said. And all at once, it dawned on Darryl that, of course, Jay had had no idea.

Jay looked out beyond Darryl at the doped-up crowd, a vast flock of zombies in crappy

Figure 78
They Performed Their Moronic Shtick.

thirty-nine-dollar flammable T-shirts emblazoned with his face, still bobbing their heads to music that was no longer even playing. Darryl saw the light in Jay's eyes dim a little and his eyes glass over, as if he weren't seeing the crowd, in fact, but were somehow gazing down on this world, on its fraught and unsettling future, on everything that lay in store for him and everyone else. It was a good look on a teenager, normally, but Darryl had never seen anyone look as lost as Jay did right then.

Darryl snapped into action. Change of plans.

Figure 79
"They Didn't Notice a Thing. But Jude Did."

This wasn't an insignificant decision. Changing plans wasn't something Darryl did lightly, ever. And there were plenty of plans left to implement, each a clever key that would unlock the next intricate plan. Some were pretty subtle, sure, like how he was going to change the spotlight to cast an unflattering color on Jude's face, revealing that he was indeed a Winter, not a Summer, like he'd always claimed to be. Others were more overt, like the drone he'd programmed to pluck the wig off Jude's head. But all of Darryl's planning work meant nothing now. It

Figure 80
He Pressed a Button on His Codpiece.

was instinct time. Not Darryl's strong suit, in part because his mother was always telling him, "Don't trust your gut, Darryl; it's just the pinworms talking." He kept his binder with him, just in case.

He dropped down through the trapdoor and scampered to the base of Rooty. He tied one end of a rope around his waist and tucked the binder into his pants. Taking a deep puff from his asthma inhaler, he told himself, "Be brave, Real Darryl." He kicked out the peg tethering the rope to the stage, shot up into the tree, and landed gracefully on one of Rooty's upper branches.

Right beside the bomb. The crowd gasped, which pleased Darryl. They were gasping at *his* peril, something that had never happened to him before.

... 45, 44, 43 ...

The view was amazing. He could see where the burned-down high school was being rebuilt, and the traffic dust rising up off the roads that circled the town, people on their way somewhere that wasn't here. Darryl had thought the sun had already set, but there it was, in the distance, the top of it just then sinking below the horizon, burning an orange and violent flame across the flat desert landscape, as if, in its refusal to go down, it would set the whole world on fire.

But just as quickly, the sun was snuffed out, and the view became terrifying. The wind picked up.

"Mickey's never been this high up," Darryl said.

The spotlight found Darryl up there, and the crowd's primitive bloodlust was kin-dled. "Jump! Jump! Jump!" they chanted.

"Oh," Jay whispered. "Mickey. No."

※

Normally, this much sustained exertion would have worn Darryl out. He was usually good for thirty seconds, max. If he was at home with Wade, for instance, engaging in enhanced horseplay, this would have been the moment Darryl's mom came in and sent Wade home with a "Darryl needs a rest. He's pooped." But his mom wasn't here to put a stop to things, and besides, he wasn't pooped at all, he had a mission, a purpose. He'd never been less pooped.

A mess of wires snaked out of the bomb and into a control-panel door on Rooty's trunk. Darryl flipped it open and flipped open his binder to a schematic titled "Stupid Tree Bomb," which he'd found in his research and was never planning on using, since exposing the band should have done the trick.

Figure 81
"'Be Brave, Real Darryl.'"

*

He flicked open a switch-blade. He sliced a couple of wires with such confidence you never would have known that until now he'd never handled a sharp knife, as his mother didn't want him using them.

From far below, Mary said to herself, "Hey, that's my blade . . . ," and indeed it was — the result of Darryl committing to doing "one thing that scares you," in this case, "take something from Mary."

Darryl began to sing.

You came in on a storm . . .

But his voice cracked and the wind picked up and swept away what little sound he'd

Figure 82
"Normally, This Much Exertion Would Have Worn Darryl Out."

✳

made. The tree branch swayed. He could hear the crowd booing. He closed his eyes. He took a deep breath. He opened his mouth and tried again.

You came in on a storm . . .

And this time, his voice didn't crack, and from far below, another voice picked up the thread.

We came together . . .

Jay! Jay was singing with no auto-tune now, his voice clear and true, and instantly quieting the crowd's boos.

Darryl: *I fell in love with your mom . . .*

Jay: *Best friends forever . . .*

Darryl: *But now . . . all I know . . . is I don't know you . . . anymore.*

Figure 83
He Flipped It Open.

✳

Darryl knew he should have rhymed "storm" with "warm" instead of that creepy line about Jay's mom, but the audience roared its approval anyway. Creepy always works better when put into songs, Darryl thought.

Darryl cut another wire.

...22...21...

❧

Mary kicked in a backbeat on the hi-hat. Jay took his turn leading the call-and-response.

Jay: *The light's so bright I got blind...*

Darryl: *Like that time I got pink eye...*

Jay: *Guess I've been saved just in time...*

Darryl: *And you didn't give me . . . stink eye . . . ?*

Jay: *'Cause . . . all I know . . . is I don't know who I am . . . anymore.*

Every phone in flashlight mode now formed an immense and dazzling constellation below Darryl. "Focus," Darryl told himself.

He snipped a few more wires.

. . . 16 . . . 15 . . .

And he sang out:

You get back to your ideals . . .

. . . 13 . . . 12 . . .

Jay: *And you can be my true friend . . .*

. . . 10 . . .

❧

According to the schematic, the last wire to cut to defuse the bomb was labeled SKIN-COLORED, and Darryl was trying to figure out if this was a trick question . . .

. . . 9 . . .

. . . when his schematic was knocked right out of his hands by a dark blur.

Mike!

The bird flew down and landed on Jude's shoulder.

They gave each other a freaky interspecies kiss. Jude was looking at Darryl, saying something, but he was too far away and Darryl couldn't hear him. He could see, though, that the fury in his eyes was flecked with hurt. There was no time to process this, since now Darryl had no binder. He had no schematic. He had no plan. He felt dizzy.

. . . 8 . . .

He kept singing—what else could he do?

Darryl: *I'll be Darryl for reals . . .*

Jay: *I won't wear spandex again . . .*

. . . 6 . . .

Darryl and Jay together: *And now . . . all I know . . .*

. . . 5 . . .

. . . is just who I am . . . forever . . . moooo . . .

. . . 4 . . .

. . . oooo . . .

. . . 3 . . .

. . . rrrrrrrre!

. . . 2 . . .

Darryl closed his eyes, and reached out with his hands,

and grabbed hold of a latte-colored wire, and cut it.

He opened his eyes. The clock had stopped.

Jay and Mary exhaled. The crowd went apeshit. Darryl let go of the branch and raised his hands in celebration. He whooped and the crowd below whooped with him. He whooped again even louder and their response was louder in return. He wobbled and reached back to steady himself, but as usual, he'd misjudged where he was in the world. He gave a small sigh of resignation.

And then he fell.

⁂

Any time he'd imagined falling out of Rooty—which had been quite often, to be honest—he was falling fast and straight down and landing with a sickening crunch.

In reality, though, while there was a lot of down, none of it was straight, or fast. His fall involved a lot of bouncing, in fact. As he bounced off one branch and then another, each bounce dislodged a highlight of his life:

Bonk: a really great toothbrush holder he got for his seventh birthday.

Crack: the time his mom accidentally bought 1 percent milk (soo creamy!).

Snap: the time he had pink eye in his left eye instead of his right eye.

Crash: the time he thought he'd found a silver denarius but it turned out to be a flattened mummified thumb.

Darryl admitted to himself that these were not great memories.

He fell on a thin, flattish branch, and for a moment the falling was over.

The crowd cheered.

He could see Jay below, watching all this unfold.

Somehow he knew that Jay could, in this moment, save him with one of his tricks, with a snap of his fingers, a good hard wink. He could see that Jay knew this, too, could see Jay taking a tentative step closer, his thumb and

forefinger poised to make that snap a reality, but Darryl whispered inside his own head, *No, don't, wait*, and he didn't know how, but Jay heard him, not only heard him but understood him, understood what Darryl had done, understood the power of sacrifice, that it was immutable and earned only through pain.

Darryl took a deep breath and let it out and then smiled at Jay, but before he could see whether or not Jay smiled back, the branch he was lying on broke, and his rush to the bottom continued.

His head hit an especially inflexible burl and he saw stars swimming in front of him, followed by a brief but brilliant supercut of his life that sparkled by . . .

The sweet sandstorm that swept Jay into town.

The crunch of sand between his teeth, which lingered for days.

The moment Jay stood up at the Flutes and Lutes Festival and brought the world to rest, brought peace to the land. The day Jay grabbed Darryl around the shoulders in the cafeteria and called him his best friend.

Darryl's hair on fire, so very hot and also so very cool.

The great song he and Jay just made up minutes ago.

The memory of the two of them at the foot of Rooty, sharing secrets, gazing up into the very air he was passing through now.

Darryl spread his arms, not in fear but in something he might have called ecstasy, if he'd ever heard anyone use the word "ecstasy" in his presence.

It dawned on him that there was, right now, however long this might last, nothing wrong with him at all—no aches, no tingling extremities, no worrying about everyone and everything. No loneliness. Nothing but freedom.

Freedom and happiness.

Figure 84
"And Then He Fell."

SPRING

Darryl, as he had imagined he would, landed with a sickening crunch.

Jay rushed to Darryl's side and cradled his head in his lap and — taking care to avoid the bubble-gum-colored snot ballooning from Darryl's nostrils — stroked his face gently.

And then Mary was there by Jay's side, holding Darryl, too. And though he couldn't see tears in her eyes, he saw, for maybe the first time ever, something in her eyes that wasn't her usual blanket disdain toward all things and all people.

She leaned in close — close enough he could feel her lips buzzing the fine hairs on his ear — and whispered to Darryl, "I always loved you."

Darryl's eye — the one still in its socket — lit up.

"Really?" he said dreamily, if a little sadly.

And then he went limp.

Jay turned to Mary. "Really?" he asked. Mary shook her head. "No," she said, "but I figured it would be nice to say so." It seemed like she was done, but with Mary you never knew. "And that song and the bomb and the fall and everything . . . that right there, that was . . . metal."

Darryl made a gurgling noise, which startled everyone, and then he died for real.

Jude could not believe what was happening, and so he took a picture to prove it was.

※

Jay was a mess. He stood to face the crowd, which had been silently watching this soap-opera moment unfold. In one elegant motion, he tore off his costume, like a stripper de-pantsing. He ripped off his tube-top tunic and used it to wipe away his mascara. Then he stormed toward the merch stands.

Jude saw him coming — really, he'd seen all this coming — and just ran. Ronnie scampered after him, knowing full well he'd sucked the situation dry.

Figure 85
"'I Always Loved You.'"

Jay started kicking over the tables, laden with swag.

A girl from the crowd shouted, "You suck, Fake Darryl!" And that was all the crowd had been waiting for. As one, they joined Jay on his rampage, pulling the stage to pieces and, in an unfortunate bit of overinterpretation, tearing Fake Darryl limb from limb.

And for the first — and what would be the last — time in his life, Jay did nothing to stop them.

Soon the crowd had torn apart everything they could — the stage, the equipment, the

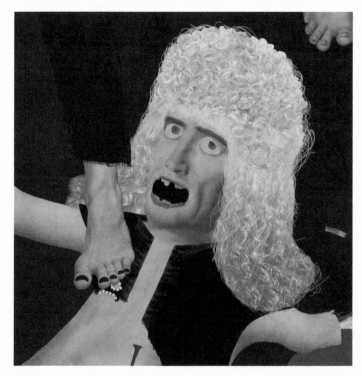

Figure 86
"'You Suck, Fake Darryl!'"

merch tables. They'd over-turned food trucks and had even tried to bring down the giant tree, which, thankfully, still stood. And then, with nothing left to destroy, the crowd slowly dispersed.

Jay stood on the remains of the stage and surveyed the destruction. In a small, dark corner of his heart, he wished it would have gone on even longer, would have raged as hot and bright as he raged inside. But he knew, too, that nothing would have satis-fied that.

As he turned to leave, he noticed something blue and plasticky on the ground, lodged

Figure 87
"There Was a Single Item Left Unchecked."

*

underneath one of Fake Darryl's butchered bits.

It was Real Darryl's binder.

Jay picked it up and gingerly paged through it. He remembered Darryl showing it to him in the tree, how his hands were shaking when he handed it over. It had changed a lot since then. What had once been just a messy collection of thoughts and emotions and loose ideals felt somehow more confident, complete. It looked less like a haphazard binder and more elegant, eloquent, like a book. He studied Darryl's pie charts and plans, worries, woes, and slightly disturbing conspiracy theories. He felt his way

through the pages and finally arrived at a sticky note that read "Life Accomplishments." There was a list of items, each with a little box beside it:

- ☑ *Climb a tree past the first branch*
- ☑ *Get a freaking job (thx Mom)*
- ☑ *Form a band that's not just me + Mary (no offense Mary!)*
- ☑ *Pierce a body part (thx Mary!)*
- ☑ *Move past Wade's betrayal/ death*
- ☑ *Feel not horrible about myself (thx Jay!)*
- ☑ *Inspire others (thx headbanging!)*
- ☑ *Jump off a park bench*
- ☑ *Play with matches/fire*
- ☑ *Make a list of life accomplishments*

There was a single item left unchecked.

- ☐ *Make Jay love me as much as I love him*

Jay unvelcroed the clip-on pen and checked the box.

The ink, he noticed, smelled like candy floss.

He velcroed the pen back in place, closed the binder, and ran his fingers over Darryl's name on the back cover. He noticed that the traced-over letters, swollen with ink, felt kind of like a scar. Jay tucked the binder into his satchel. He thought — though maybe this was the adrenaline talking — that the satchel felt lighter now than it had before.

Or maybe it wasn't the satchel that felt lighter. Maybe it was Jay. If anyone had been there to see it, and they were paying real close attention and also were standing at a very particular angle, they might have said he was kind of hovering, suspended from an invisible string, not off the ground but not on it either. Jay slung the satchel over his shoulder and walk-glided away, sort of a moonwalk, but, like, going forward.

If Darryl had seen it, he might have said, *Smooth move*, then after a slight dramatic pause, *Ex-Lax!* And then they would have laughed.

❧

Figure 88
"Sort of a Moonwalk, but, Like, Going Forward"

‡

YOFON. LEGENDS NEVER DIE!

U SUCKED

DARRYL
HE WAS KINDA COOL

TREE OF LIFE   L WILLO'UE KISSED U

JUDE W   ROOT   RIP

MISS YA

Acknowledgments

The Book of Darryl went through several incarnations
before settling into this earthly form. It's based
on an online series of the same name, which was
generously supported by the Canada Media Fund
and Screen Australia.

The creative team behind *The Book of Darryl* is composed
of The Goggles (Paul Shoebridge and Michael Simons),
Matthew Bate, and the animator Scorpion Dagger, aka
James Kerr. Ryan Battistuzzi set the whole thing to
bitchin' music.

Additional wordsmithing by
Manuel Gonzales, Bruce Grierson, and
J. B. MacKinnon. Additional design by Alex Merto.
Editorial shepherding by Sean McDonald.

So many others helped Darryl on his way. His mom,
naturally, but also Rebecca Summerton, Closer
Productions, Mike Robbins / Helios Design Labs,
BVA, Sebastian Strakowicz, Andy Hughes, and, of
course, all of our long-suffering partners and pals.

Darryl thanks you all, and we do, too.

A Note About the Authors

The Goggles are Paul Shoebridge and Michael Simons, creators who have spent their professional lives telling stories in compelling new ways. Their interactive documentary, *Welcome to Pine Point*, received more than a dozen international awards. They are coauthors of the book *I Live Here*, and their work has been featured on CNN and MTV, and in documentaries for the BBC, PBS, and Dutch National Television.

Closer Productions' Matt Bate is a writer, director, and producer working across drama, documentary, and VR. His debut feature film, *Shut Up, Little Man!*, premiered in competition at Sundance 2011, and his sophomore film, *Sam Klemke's Time Machine*, was selected for Sundance New Frontier 2014.

James Kerr is a digital artist based in Montreal who is best known for his animated GIF project Scorpion Dagger, in which he mixes cutouts from various paintings from art history to comment on our modern age and pop culture in general.